# Chapter O.

The first thing Sophie noticed about the cottage was the silence. Not just the absence of traffic or city buzz, but a deeper, fuller kind of silence, as though the world itself had stopped breathing. Her boots crunched over gravel as she stepped out of the car, the sound sharp and sudden in the stillness. The January sky was a flat sheet of grey above her, casting a pale, lifeless light over the land. Everything felt dulled, like the world had been washed in ash and left to dry. The cottage stood squat and stubborn at the end of the long dirt track, its windows dark, its roof sagging slightly under the weight of age and neglect. Tufts of moss clung to the stone like old bruises, and ivy crept up one side as if trying to strangle it back into the earth.

She pulled her coat tighter around her and glanced over at the removal van idling behind her. The driver, a man with too many piercings for a cold morning and an attitude she hadn't appreciated on the two-hour journey from Lincoln, leaned against the cab and lit a cigarette. He didn't offer to help. Sophie didn't expect him to. His music had been too loud, his eyes too uninterested. For the last leg of the drive, she'd turned her face to the window and pretended not to exist.

"All here, then," she muttered to herself. Her voice sounded small.

The cottage had once belonged to her father's aunt—Elsie Hale—a woman Sophie had met only a handful of times as a child, always in brief, stiff visits where the conversation never flowed and affection felt absent. Elsie had been the kind of woman who smelled of lavender and mothballs, who offered lemon biscuits in tins too dented to close properly. Her father rarely spoke of Aunt Elsie, and her mother even less. It was only after the funeral, when Sophie had been summoned by a solicitor she'd never met, that she discovered the cottage had been left to her. Just her. No explanation. No note. Just a set of tarnished brass keys in a yellow envelope and a crumpled map with a red X where the property stood. No sentimental letter, no mention in the will of why it was hers.

## The Weight of Silence

Inside, the air smelled of dust and time. The last time the place had seen life must have been years ago. Plastic sheets covered the furniture, and a brittle chill settled into Sophie's bones as she stepped over the threshold. Her breath came in small puffs, visible in the weak light. The floorboards creaked beneath her feet like reluctant ghosts waking up after years of silence. The silence inside was different from the silence outside. Outside, it was the hush of a winter landscape, vast and indifferent. Inside, it was the silence of abandonment, a heavy cloak woven from forgotten whispers and unfulfilled dreams. Every creak of the old house seemed to amplify it, making the emptiness even more profound. Sophie shivered, though it wasn't just the cold. It was the vast, echoing space that seemed to swallow her whole.

The hallway was narrow, the wallpaper a faded rose pattern curling away from the walls like forgotten petals. She pulled the sheet off a small wooden console and ran a finger across the surface, leaving a trail in the dust. The console itself felt ancient, its dark wood worn smooth by countless touches from hands long gone. She imagined Elsie, perhaps, placing her keys there, or setting down a cup of tea. These small, mundane details were all that remained of a life lived within these walls. The faded wallpaper, with its delicate, almost ghostly rose pattern, seemed to cling precariously to the plaster, threatening to peel away entirely at the slightest disturbance. It was a visual metaphor for the fragile hold the past had on the present in this house.

"Christ," she said under her breath. "What the hell am I doing here?"

She had asked herself that question a hundred times since she signed the paperwork. Since she had packed up the last box in the flat she once shared with Daniel. Since she had told her boss she needed time away from the London office and the marketing job that no longer made her feel anything at all. It was the winter of 2010, and at thirty-six years old, Sophie felt a weary decade older than her actual years, driven away from everything that used to be her life, clutching the keys to a place she didn't know, inherited from a woman she barely remembered. The question wasn't rhetorical; it was a desperate plea for an answer that she couldn't articulate. Her life in London, once so vibrant and clearly defined, had become a dull, colourless blur. The marketing job, which had once seemed like the pinnacle of her ambitions, now felt like a soul-sucking treadmill. And Daniel... Daniel was a ghost, a presence that still haunted the edges of her consciousness, despite the divorce being final. This cottage, this unexpected inheritance, felt like a last-ditch attempt at escape, a desperate gamble in a game she hadn't chosen to play.

Maybe it was madness. Maybe it was survival. Maybe the two weren't so different. She found a strange comfort in that thought, a perverse kind of logic that suggested her current drastic measures were not a sign of a breakdown, but rather a primal instinct to stay afloat.

The living room was small but had good bones—as the estate agent had said with a tone too cheery for what had clearly been a neglected home. A fireplace sat at the centre of the far wall, its iron grate rusted and cold. Built-in bookshelves flanked it, still half-stocked with yellowing paperbacks and hardbacks that had seen better decades. The books smelled of age, their pages brittle and sun-bleached. Sophie ran her hand over the spines, the faint scent of decaying paper and dust rising to meet her. It was a comforting smell in a way, familiar from countless hours spent in old libraries and second-hand bookshops. She pulled out a few titles – faded classics, forgotten romances, and a surprising number of gardening guides. Elsie, it seemed, had a practical side. On one shelf sat a framed photo turned facedown. Sophie picked it up and wiped the glass with her sleeve.

A woman in her early twenties stared back at her, dark-haired, solemn-eyed. Her resemblance to Sophie was uncanny. The same high cheekbones, the same serious set to the mouth, even the slight asymmetry of the left eyebrow. The photo was black and white, the edges frayed, suggesting it had been handled often, perhaps carried in a wallet or kept by a bedside. It was a stark, almost unsettling resemblance. Sophie felt a jolt of recognition, as if she were looking at a younger version of herself, or perhaps a reflection in a warped mirror.

"Aunt Elsie," she murmured.

She placed the photo upright again and took a step back. A strange sensation bloomed low in her stomach—not quite fear, not quite familiarity. Just... something. It was a sense of connection, a faint tremor of recognition that transcended the simple act of looking at a photograph. It was as if Elsie, even in death, was reaching out, a silent greeting across the chasm of time. She shook it off. Probably just the cold and the loneliness already playing tricks. But the feeling lingered, a subtle hum beneath the surface of her consciousness.

## Echoes of a Life

Behind her, the front door banged open and the removal men filed in, muttering to each other, stamping snow and mud into the hallway. The sudden intrusion of noise and activity was jarring after the profound silence. Sophie flinched, the spell broken. The outside world, with its grimy boots and loud conversations, was here. She let them carry in her life, box by box, feeling each delivery echo in the hollow space around her. A cracked lamp. A box of kitchen utensils. Her plants, wrapped in newspaper like broken memories. Each item, once so carefully chosen and loved in her London flat, now seemed alien and diminished in the vast, cold emptiness of the cottage. They looked like refugees, shipwrecked remnants of a life that had been abruptly overturned.

By the time they left, the grey sky had darkened to charcoal. The silence, when it returned, was even deeper, punctuated only by the distant hum of the removal van fading into the winter evening. She made herself a cup of tea from a camping stove she'd brought, having been warned the electricity might take a day to reconnect. The water boiled with a quiet hiss, and the faint scent of tea leaves mingled with the pervasive smell of dust and old paper. She sat cross-legged on the floor in front of the fireplace, her coat still on, the cup warming her fingers. The tea was weak, but the warmth was a small comfort against the encroaching chill. She didn't bother unpacking anything else. Not yet. The thought of sorting through boxes, of trying to impose order on this chaos, felt utterly overwhelming. She just sat there, the light fading, the room swallowing the silence once more. The last vestiges of daylight retreated from the windows, leaving the room cloaked in a deepening gloom.

Outside, wind whispered through the trees. It was a mournful sound, like a lament carried on the cold air, rising and falling in rhythmic sighs. Somewhere nearby, a fox barked. The sound startled her at first, sharp in the hush, but then it faded, becoming part of the atmosphere, part of the wild stillness around her. It was a sound of life, wild and untamed, a reminder that even in this forgotten corner of the world, there was a vibrant ecosystem at play.

She thought about calling someone. Her sister, always ready with a witty remark or a sympathetic ear. Her father, who would undoubtedly offer practical advice she didn't want to hear. Her friend, Claire, who had begged her not to disappear up north like a war widow in a Brontë novel. Claire's words echoed in her mind, a playful jab that now felt strangely prescient. But she didn't. The urge to explain herself had long since drained away. What was there to say, anyway? "I've run away to a dilapidated cottage I inherited from an aunt I barely knew, and I have no idea why"? No, silence felt easier, safer.

Instead, she reached for the small box marked "keepsakes." Most of what she owned had been purged in the divorce—an oddly cathartic process that left her feeling both hollowed out and free. The physical act of shedding possessions had been a painful but necessary cleansing. This box, however, held the fragments of her true self, the pieces she couldn't bear to part with. She opened the box and pulled out a notebook, her old writing journal. Pages half-filled with thoughts and starts of things she never finished. Scribbles of poetry. Lists of words she liked. Half-formed stories that stopped mid-sentence, abandoned like fledgling birds pushed too soon from the nest.

She hadn't written properly in years. The demands of her career, the complexities of her marriage, and later, the raw grief of its dissolution, had stifled her creative impulse. But just holding the notebook grounded her. The familiar weight of it in her hands, the scent of old paper and ink, it was a tangible link to a part of herself she had almost forgotten. It was a quiet promise, a whisper of a possibility that maybe, just maybe, this solitude, this stillness, could rekindle that lost spark. She traced the faint lines of her own handwriting on the first page, a ghost of her past self reaching out to her present.

## A New Dawn, A Hidden Past

By the time she unpacked her bed and wrestled the mattress onto the creaky frame in the upstairs room, it was past ten. Her limbs ached from the cold and the weight of the day, a satisfying fatigue that spoke of physical exertion rather than mental exhaustion. She lay in the dark, the only sound the occasional creak of wood settling and the soft rattle of wind against the panes. Somewhere, something thudded faintly. A branch? An animal? Her imagination already running riot? The house, despite its age, was beginning to speak to her, its whispers and groans forming a strange nocturnal symphony.

Sleep didn't come easy. Her mind, accustomed to the constant hum of city life, struggled to adjust to the profound quiet. Every shadow seemed to deepen, every creak to echo. She drifted in and out of a restless slumber, images of Elsie's solemn face, the faded rose wallpaper, and the vast, empty fields swirling through her dreams.

Morning broke slow and pale. A timid light filtered through the thin curtains, painting the room in muted shades of grey and silver. Sophie rose early, dressed in layers – thick wool socks, an old jumper, her coat still on. The cottage air remained stubbornly cold, clinging to everything like a damp shroud. She wandered the property with a mug of lukewarm instant coffee, the bitter taste a sharp contrast to the soft dawn light. The cottage stood on the edge of a forgotten orchard. Gnarled apple trees stretched their bare arms into the sky, their roots thick and coiled above ground like sleeping serpents. Dead leaves and frost clung to the earth like a shroud, a silent testament to the winter's grip. A crumbling stone wall edged the boundary, its stones scattered and moss-covered, and beyond it, open fields reached for the horizon, a vast expanse of muted browns and greys under the soft light.

She stood still for a long moment, letting the cold bite at her cheeks. The air was crisp, clean, carrying the faint scent of damp earth and woodsmoke from a distant farm. For the first time in months, she didn't feel overwhelmed. She felt... present. Not pulled backward by regret or forward by fear. The weight of her past, the specter of Daniel, the disappointment of her career – all of it seemed to recede, held at bay by the raw, elemental beauty of the landscape. There was a sense of quiet acceptance, a surrender to the immediate moment. This was here, now. And for the first time in a long time, that felt like enough.

Inside, she began to explore in earnest. She opened every drawer, every cupboard, cataloguing a life frozen in time. In the kitchen, cracked china cups with hairline cracks sat alongside tarnished silver cutlery. In the pantry, jars of forgotten preserves, their contents long since turned to dust, lined dusty shelves. The bedroom held simple, heavy wooden furniture, and a worn quilt folded neatly at the foot of the bed. Elsie's possessions were sparse, practical, hinting at a life lived with quiet austerity. Letters half-written, their ink faded to sepia, lay tucked into a desk drawer. Dried flowers, brittle and colourless, were pressed between the pages of an old hymn book. The house was a quiet museum, each item a relic, each room a chapter in Elsie's untold story. In the attic, she found boxes full of newspapers from the 1940s, their headlines screaming of war and sacrifice, a chilling reminder of the world Elsie had lived through. Old linens, wrapped in mothballed cloth, smelled faintly of lavender, a last whisper of Elsie's scent. A cracked mirror, its silvering peeling, tilted awkwardly against the beams, reflecting a distorted image of her own solemn face.

## The Hidden Letters

But it was in the smallest upstairs bedroom—what must once have been a nursery or a sewing room—where she found something strange. The room was sparse, almost empty, with only a narrow, single bed pushed against one wall and a small, warped wardrobe. The air in this room felt different, a subtle shift in the heavy silence.

The floor creaked as she stepped across the room, the sound amplified in the stillness. She pulled open the warped wardrobe, its hinges groaning in protest, and peered inside. Empty. A faint smell of cedar and old cloth lingered. But as she turned, her foot caught on an uneven board near the corner of the room. It was a subtle give, barely perceptible, but enough to catch her attention.

She knelt, pressing her hand against the floor. One plank, near the corner, felt different. Loose. Her fingers traced the edge of the plank, feeling a slight gap where it met its neighbour. A spark of curiosity ignited within her, chasing away the lingering chill. This wasn't just a loose board; it felt deliberate.

She fetched a screwdriver from her unpacked toolbox, its metal cold and sharp in her hand. Carefully, she inserted the tip into the narrow gap and pried. Dust puffed into the air, a miniature explosion of particles dancing in the pale light from the window. The plank lifted with a soft sigh of protest, revealing a shallow space beneath. And within it—a bundle of old papers, tied with a red ribbon now faded to rust.

Her heart jumped. It was a visceral reaction, a sudden surge of adrenaline that tightened her chest. This wasn't just old junk; this was something hidden, something secret. The sheer anticipation of what she might find made her breath catch in her throat.

She pulled the bundle free and sat down on the edge of the narrow bed, the springs groaning softly under her weight. Her fingers, usually steady, trembled slightly as she untied the ribbon. It disintegrated in her fingers, a fragile testament to the passage of time. Inside were letters. Dozens of them. Stacked neatly, almost reverently, as if someone had placed them there with great care. All addressed to the same name:

"My Dearest Thomas."

Her fingers trembled slightly as she unfolded the first one. The paper was thin, brittle, and smelled faintly of lavender and something else – a faint, almost metallic scent, like old ink and forgotten emotions. The handwriting was neat, slanted, unfamiliar, yet it exuded a certain grace, a confident hand that belied the urgency of the words. But the words— they were full of longing, urgency, and secrets. They spoke of wartime, of danger, of meetings in orchards under the cloak of darkness, of whispered plans exchanged in hurried moments. The voice was passionate. Brave. Afraid. It was Elsie's voice, not the reserved, lavender-scented woman of her childhood memories, but a vibrant, living woman, full of fierce emotion.

Sophie read the letter three times, her skin prickling with goosebumps despite the cold. Each word painted a vivid picture in her mind, transporting her to a different time, a different life. She saw Elsie, young and passionate, meeting her forbidden lover under the cover of night, risking everything for a stolen moment. She felt the fear, the desperation, the desperate hope that permeated every line. The letters were a raw, unfiltered glimpse into Elsie's hidden world, a world Sophie had never known existed.

And when she finally looked up, something had changed. The house no longer felt empty. It felt like it was waiting. Waiting for her to discover its secrets, to unlock its past. The silence was no longer a void, but a hushed anticipation, a living presence that vibrated with untold stories. Sophie felt a profound shift within her, a connection not just to Elsie, but to the very fabric of the cottage itself. It was no longer just a place she had inherited; it was a mystery, a puzzle, and she, Sophie, was its reluctant, yet undeniably eager, detective. The isolation she had sought now felt less like an escape and more like an invitation. An invitation to unearth a hidden history, and perhaps, in doing so, to finally find her own place in the world.

# Chapter Two

Lincolnshire, Spring 1941

The train whistled its mournful farewell, a long, drawn-out cry that seemed to carry the last echoes of London with it as it pulled away from the small country station. Elsie Hale stood alone on the platform, a single, worn leather suitcase at her feet, feeling the heavy scent of coal smoke linger in the air, clinging to her coat, her hair, even the very lining of her lungs. It was a smell utterly alien to the crisp, clean air she now breathed, a harsh reminder of the sprawling, bustling city she had left behind. In one hand, she clutched her government-issued papers – stark, official documents that felt both immensely important and utterly insignificant in the vastness of this new landscape. In the other, a folded letter, creased and softened from anxious handling, the one that had told her precisely where to report for work and, more importantly, who to ask for. The paper felt thin, almost insubstantial, a fragile link to the life she was about to embark upon.

The silence that descended after the train's departure was profound, almost deafening. It wasn't the agitated, buzzing quiet of a Sunday afternoon in Kensington, but a deep, encompassing stillness, broken only by the rustle of unseen leaves and the distant bleating of sheep. It made her own breathing sound loud, almost intrusive. Elsie adjusted the grip on her suitcase, the worn leather digging slightly into her palm. Her smart London boots, chosen for pavement and polite calls, already felt inadequate on the coarse gravel of the platform.

"Land Army, Miss Hale?" a voice called from behind, cutting through the vast quiet like a sharp, clean knife.

She turned, startled. A tall woman stood waiting near a parked tractor, an ancient machine that looked as though it had seen decades of hard labour. The woman wore a thick wool coat that appeared impervious to the chill, and a practical headscarf tightly bound around her hair, leaving not a single strand out of place. Her boots were caked in mud, a testament to a morning already spent wrestling with the earth, and a no-nonsense expression was carved deeply into her sun-worn face. Her eyes, a startling shade of blue, assessed Elsie with an almost clinical efficiency.

"Yes, ma'am. Elsie Hale," Elsie replied, her voice sounding thin and prim in her own ears, far too refined for this rugged landscape. She straightened her shoulders, attempting to project an air of confidence she didn't quite feel.

The woman gave a brisk nod, her gaze unwavering. "I'm Margaret Tully. You'll be posted at Ravenswick Farm. Just over a mile's walk, I'm afraid. This way." She gestured with a gloved hand towards a winding, unpaved track that disappeared into the muted landscape. There was no offer of help with the suitcase, no softening of the brisk tone. Elsie understood immediately that sentimentality was not a currency traded in these parts.

Elsie picked up her suitcase, its weight suddenly seeming immense. The handle, usually a comfortable curve, felt like a blunt instrument in her hand. She fell into step behind Margaret, who set a surprisingly swift pace. Her boots, smart and new that morning, were already pinching mercilessly at her toes, each step sending a jolt of discomfort up her shins. Her coat, a stylish wool blend that had offered sufficient warmth for a London street, offered little protection against the damp, biting wind that rolled unchecked across the flat, open fields. It seemed to seep right into her bones, a cold that was both physical and strangely, profoundly, isolating. She missed the comforting, oppressive closeness of London's buildings, the way they huddled together against the elements. Here, everything was exposed.

They walked in near silence, the only sounds the crunch of their boots on the gravel track and the distant caw of rooks. Margaret spoke only to point out landmarks, her voice devoid of inflection: a flooded ditch where sheep liked to get stuck, its dark water reflecting the grey sky like a broken mirror; a lopsided fence post someone had hit with a tractor, a splintered testament to agricultural mishaps; the old orchard that hadn't borne decent fruit in years, its gnarled, skeletal branches reaching like twisted claws towards the sky. Elsie listened, trying to imprint these unfamiliar way-markers onto her memory, knowing they were now crucial to her existence here. Each landmark felt like a cryptic clue in a puzzle she had yet to understand.

"You'll bunk in the cottage beside the main house. You'll have the room to yourself unless they send another girl," Margaret explained, her voice as flat and unyielding as the landscape around them. There was no warmth in her tone, no welcoming gesture. It was simply a statement of fact, a logistical detail in the vast, relentless machinery of wartime agriculture. Elsie felt a flicker of relief at the prospect of solitude, even if it came wrapped in such a chilly package. After the constant clamour of London, the shared lodgings, the pervasive sense of being constantly observed, the idea of having a space, however small, entirely to herself, was a precious one.

When they finally arrived at Ravenswick Farm, Elsie paused at the edge of the orchard. The trees were ancient things, hunched and skeletal against the perpetually grey sky, their bare branches interwoven like the arthritic fingers of giants. They seemed to absorb all the light around them, casting long, mournful shadows even in the dim daylight. The farm buildings ahead were modest, practical. The main house, a low-slung stone building, had cracked windowpanes that looked like weeping eyes, and its brickwork was stained with the grime of decades. An old barn leaned precariously against the wind, its timbers groaning, like an old drunk perpetually on the verge of collapse. Everything here spoke of endurance, of harsh realities, of a beauty that was stark and unadorned.

The cottage Margaret showed her into was small but felt solid, a comforting anchor in the shifting landscape. It contained one bedroom, barely large enough for a single bed and a small chest of drawers. A sitting area with a fireplace, its hearth stained black with years of soot, promised a meagre source of warmth against the relentless cold. A tiny kitchen, its air smelling faintly of damp earth and the lingering ghost of potatoes, completed the sparse living quarters. There were cracks in the walls, fine lines that spider-webbed across the plaster like ancient maps, and the soot stains around the hearth indeed confirmed the cottage's long history of providing warmth. But despite its imperfections, its undeniable air of neglect, it was hers, for now. A temporary haven in a world turned upside down. It was a space to be alone, to breathe, to simply be.

Margaret's instructions were as blunt and functional as the tools Elsie would soon be wielding. "Water's from the pump outside. You'll be mucking out, feeding the hens, collecting eggs, fixing fences. No whining, no airs. We all work hard here." It was a clear delineation of her new life, a complete departure from the polite, paper-strewn world of a solicitor's office. Elsie absorbed the litany of chores, nodding, her resolve firming with each utilitarian command. "Yes, ma'am," she replied, her voice stronger now, a faint tremor of defiance in its newfound steadiness.

As Margaret turned to leave, her hand already on the cottage door, she added a final, seemingly innocuous warning. "And don't wander too far into the orchard," she said, her eyes briefly flicking towards the gnarled trees. "Stray roots and rabbit holes. Easy to twist an ankle." Elsie nodded again, filing the information away. At the time, it seemed like nothing more than a practical caution, a small piece of advice in a vast sea of new directives. She couldn't know then how profoundly significant that gnarled, neglected orchard would become to her, how it would weave itself into the very fabric of her future.

The Rhythm of the Earth
The work was backbreaking. Every muscle in Elsie's body protested in a chorus of aches and stiffness by the end of each day. Her soft, uncalloused hands, more accustomed to the delicate click of typewriter keys and the rustle of legal documents, quickly became blistered and raw. The mornings came cold and early, a relentless alarm clock of biting wind and muted light. The sun rarely warmed the earth before midday, and even then, its weak rays offered little comfort against the pervasive damp and chill. Elsie, a typist at a solicitor's office in Kensington before volunteering, had considered herself an efficient and capable woman. But here, her skills felt utterly irrelevant. Her hands, so adept at filing letters and composing formal correspondence, seemed

stubbornly ill-suited to lifting hay bales that pricked and scratched, to hauling heavy buckets of water from the pump, to wrestling with recalcitrant hens.

Her first week left her blistered, bruised, and bone-weary. She discovered muscles she hadn't known existed, and her evenings were spent with aching limbs, the pervasive smell of farm earth clinging to her skin and clothes. Yet at night, as she sat by the faint glow of the fire in her small cottage, sipping a cup of watery tea that did little to truly warm her, and losing herself in the pages of a borrowed book – often a worn novel left behind by a previous Land Girl – she felt a quiet satisfaction she had never known in London. It was a different kind of tired, a deeper, more fundamental exhaustion that settled into her bones, but one that felt earned. A day's honest labour, the direct result visible in a tidied pen or a full basket of eggs.

She liked the solitude. It was a preference that had always been quietly present in her, a subtle leaning towards introspection that London, with its ceaseless demands and social expectations, had never quite allowed. Here, in the quiet solitude of her own small space, she found a strange kind of freedom. No one asked her about the past, about why a young woman from Kensington would volunteer for such a harsh existence. No one delved into the unspoken reasons that had driven her from the comfortable, predictable life she'd left behind. There was no need for explanations, no expectations to live up to. She was simply Elsie, the Land Girl. And that was enough.

She began keeping a journal. It wasn't a diary of deep confessions or grand aspirations, but small, meticulous observations: weather notes, painstakingly recorded in a neat, careful hand; how many eggs she'd gathered that morning, the specific shade of a sunrise, a particularly stubborn sheep. Sometimes, she would simply transcribe a witty remark Margaret had made at lunch, or a detail about a new calf. It made her feel tethered, connected to the tangible reality of her days, a small anchor in the vast, uncertain ocean of the war. It was a way to process, to observe, to simply record. The act of writing, the scratch of the pen on paper, provided a quiet rhythm to her evenings.

A Quiet Introduction

It was on her twelfth day that she saw him. The sun, a rare, pale disc in the watery sky, was beginning its slow descent, painting the western horizon in muted shades of peach and grey. She was collecting kindling near the orchard's edge, her arms already laden with fallen branches, when a figure emerged from the dense tangle of trees. He seemed to materialize out of the shadows, moving with an almost preternatural quietness. He wore an army-issue greatcoat, its rough wool a darker silhouette against the fading light, his collar upturned against the chill. A cap was pulled low over dark, almost black, hair, obscuring most of his face, but Elsie caught a glimpse of a strong jawline, a slight stubble. He moved like someone used to staying unnoticed, like a shadow flitting between the trees, a part of the landscape rather than an intruder upon it.

When their eyes met across the fading light, a jolt, subtle yet distinct, passed through Elsie. His eyes, though shadowed by the cap, were intense, a dark, intelligent gaze that held hers for only a moment. He gave a small, almost imperceptible nod, a brief acknowledgement, then kept walking, his stride even and unhurried, towards the farm buildings. He didn't speak. He didn't linger. He simply passed by, a fleeting presence that left a curious impression on Elsie's mind.

Later that evening, at dinner in the farmhouse kitchen – a bustling, often chaotic affair with the smell of roasting meat and damp wool – Elsie found herself unable to shake the image of the quiet man in the greatcoat. The memory of his silent presence, his brief, intense gaze, played in her mind, a subtle counterpoint to the lively chatter around her. She waited for a lull in the conversation, then, feigning casual curiosity, asked Margaret who he was.

Margaret, her sleeves rolled up, her hands perpetually busy, spoon hovering over a bubbling pot of stew, paused. "Thomas Ashford," she said, her tone as matter-of-fact as ever, as though stating the most obvious thing in the world. "Stays in the barracks two miles over but comes by to help with repairs. Used to live round here before the war. Quiet sort." She shrugged, resuming her stirring, as if the topic was of little consequence.

"Ashford," Elsie repeated thoughtfully, testing the name on her tongue. It sounded strong, grounded, like the land itself. "Does he live nearby?"

Margaret gave another dismissive shrug. "Grew up on a farm not far from here, I think. Lost his parents young. Keeps to himself mostly. Good with his hands, though." She added the last part almost as an afterthought, a grudging compliment.

Elsie hesitated, her fork poised over her plate, a piece of potato suddenly unappetizing. She felt an inexplicable urge to know more about this man, this silent figure who had emerged from the orchard. She took a breath, then asked the question that had been nagging at her, a question that felt both impertinent and entirely necessary. "Why isn't he overseas? Most men his age are." The air in the kitchen seemed to thicken slightly, the clatter of pots and pans seeming to quiet. It was a question that hung heavy in the air for many families, a constant, painful reminder of the war's insatiable appetite for young men.

Margaret paused again, her spoon still hovering over the pot of stew, her gaze now fixed on Elsie, sharper than before. Her expression was unreadable, a mixture of assessment and perhaps a touch of weariness. "He was," she said, her voice dropping slightly, losing some of its usual briskness. "Went over early in the war. Dunkirk nearly took him. Shrapnel to the leg, lucky to walk again. They sent him back here to recover. He's still on the books, just not fit for combat yet. Helps out where he can." The words were delivered without flourish, a simple statement of brutal fact. The name 'Dunkirk' hung in the air, a sombre word that carried the weight of mass evacuation, of narrow escapes, of unimaginable horror. Elsie absorbed that in silence, the image of the quiet man now overlaid with a new layer of vulnerability and trauma. She glanced instinctively towards the window, where the orchard, now a dark, impenetrable mass, stretched into the deepening dusk. She imagined him there, moving through its shadows, carrying the unspoken burdens of that distant, terrible beach.

Stolen Moments, Shared Quiet
Their meetings became more frequent after that, though rarely planned. They were often chance encounters, fleeting moments stolen from the relentless rhythm of farm life. Once, in the early morning, Elsie found him fixing a broken fence post at the far end of a field, his sleeves rolled up

despite the cold, his forearms strong and flecked with mud. The muscles in his back rippled beneath his thin shirt as he worked, his movements economical and precise. He didn't seem to notice her at first, entirely absorbed in his task. Another time, she passed him in the orchard itself, a flash of dark green coat against the grey-brown of the trees, and he tipped his cap with a soft, almost imperceptible "Morning." His voice was low, gravelly, a sound that resonated deep within her. He would be gone before she could formulate a response, leaving only the echo of his presence.

They spoke properly for the first time when he found her in the old barn, struggling in the dim light to repair a loose latch on a feed bin. Her fingers, still clumsy from the cold, fumbled with the rusted metal, her patience wearing thin. A shadow fell across her work, and a voice, quiet and unexpected, made her jump, a small cry escaping her lips.

"Try turning the hinge instead of forcing it," he said, his voice closer than she expected. He hadn't announced himself, simply appeared.

She spun around, her heart thudding, a flush of embarrassment rising in her cheeks. He stood there, unmoving, his dark eyes watching her with a calm, almost unnerving intensity. Without waiting for a response, he stepped forward, his movements fluid and unhesitating. He gently took the tool, a heavy wrench, from her hand, his fingers brushing hers, a brief, surprising warmth radiating from his touch. With a few deft, precise turns, the rusted latch clicked into place with satisfying finality.

"Thank you," she said, her voice still a little breathless, the embarrassment lingering. His proximity, the quiet competence of his hands, unnerved her slightly.

He straightened, handing the wrench back to her. "Not much use having hands if you don't lend them now and then," he said simply, his voice devoid of any boastfulness or condescension. There was a quiet sincerity in his tone that disarmed her.

She noticed then that he had a kindness about him, a subtle gentleness that softened the guardedness in his dark eyes. It was a quality that contradicted his quiet, almost remote demeanour. There was a faint scar near his left temple, almost hidden by his dark hair, and she wondered, briefly, if it was a remnant of Dunkirk. His gaze, though intense, held no judgment, only a quiet observation.

Over the next weeks, their encounters, once purely accidental, began to take on a subtle, unspoken rhythm. They began to talk more, in stolen minutes between chores, in brief glances exchanged across a muddy field. Sometimes, it was a shared apple beneath the sheltering branches of the orchard trees, its crisp sweetness a small luxury. He spoke little of the war, his answers brief and often evasive, only saying that he wasn't due back to France until autumn, a looming deadline that hung unspoken between them. He asked her about London, his interest genuine, prompting memories of bustling streets and red buses that now felt like a dream. He asked about books, about music, about the life she had led before the war swept her to this remote corner of England.

He liked to listen. His dark eyes would watch her as she spoke, absorbing every word, every nuance, with a quiet intensity that made her feel truly heard, truly seen. She liked to talk. With him, the words flowed easily, unburdened by the expectations or judgments she had so often felt in her former life. She found herself confiding small details, observations about the farm, reflections on her newfound solitude. It was a comfortable exchange, a quiet equilibrium.

It was the orchard that became their place. Amid its tangled branches and gnarled trunks, where the spring leaves were beginning to unfurl in delicate shades of green, they found something untouched by the war, a small sanctuary in a world consumed by conflict. The ancient trees seemed to absorb their whispered conversations, to hold their shared secrets in their very bark. The air there always felt different, a little cooler, a little more still, imbued with the scent of damp earth and the promise of future blossoms.

One evening, as the sun dropped low and gold on the horizon, painting the sky in fiery hues that bled into soft lavender, they stood closer than usual. The light filtered through the budding leaves of the apple trees, dappling their faces with shifting patterns of light and shadow. The silence between them was no longer an emptiness, but a palpable presence, charged with unspoken emotions. He reached for her hand, his fingers brushing against hers, but then hesitated, his gaze dropping to their almost-touching hands. He seemed to hold his breath, a faint tension in his shoulders.

"Elsie," he said softly, his voice a low murmur, barely audible above the gentle rustle of the wind through the branches. "I think about you. All the time."

Her breath hitched in her throat, a small, involuntary gasp. A warmth spread through her, radiating from her chest, chasing away the chill of the evening. A genuine smile bloomed on her face, a rare, unburdened expression. "I know," she whispered, her voice equally soft, almost a confession. "I think about you, too."

He gave her hand a gentle squeeze, a brief, tender pressure that sent a shiver through her, then, with a sigh that was almost imperceptible, he let it go. It was a moment of exquisite tension, of longing held in check by unspoken fears and the undeniable realities of their world. She watched him walk back through the orchard, his silhouette growing smaller against the darkening sky, her heart fluttering in her chest like a trapped bird. They weren't ready for more. Not yet. The shadow of his return to France, the constant threat of the war, cast a long, cold pall over everything. To ask for more, to demand more, felt selfish, almost reckless, in such uncertain times.

A Secret Seed

That night, back in the quiet sanctuary of her cottage, with the fire casting dancing shadows on the walls and the wind sighing softly outside, Elsie found her journal. The simple act of holding the familiar leather-bound book, the scent of its pages, provided a quiet comfort. But tonight, her thoughts were not for weather notes or egg counts. Her mind was brimming with Thomas, with his quiet strength, his gentle eyes, the lingering memory of his touch. The unspoken words, the ones they couldn't yet utter, pressed at her, demanding release.

She uncapped her ink bottle, dipped her pen, and began to write. Not in her journal, but on a separate, crisp sheet of paper, chosen with a deliberate, almost ritualistic care.

"My Dearest Thomas," she began, the words flowing from her pen, imbued with all the longing and apprehension she felt. "The war may take you back across the sea, to places I cannot imagine, to dangers I can only fear. But these words will remain here, in the earth, beneath the floorboards, between the pages of this place. They will be a testament to what we are, to what we might become. Until you return. Until I can speak them aloud again, without fear, without the shadow of this terrible conflict hanging over us."

She wrote rapidly, furiously, filling the page with a rush of emotion, a desperate attempt to capture the fleeting, precious essence of their connection. She folded the letter with care, then tucked it into a plain envelope, pressing the flap down firmly. She stood, walked over to her narrow bed, and knelt beside it. Her fingers found the familiar slight give in the floorboard near the corner. With a quiet grunt of effort, she pried it up, dust puffing softly into the air. Beneath the board was a shallow, dark space. She slid the envelope into the hidden cavity, pushing it to the very back, as if the darkness itself would protect its contents. Then she carefully replaced the floorboard, pressing it down until it settled with a soft click.

It was a small act of defiance, a quiet rebellion against the chaos of the world. A tiny, precious seed of hope planted in the heart of her solitary cottage. She would write dozens more letters, each one a whispered confession, a secret chronicle of her love for him, a desperate plea for his safe return. Each one hidden away, a testament to the fragile, precious thing they were building amidst the destruction.

And in time, as the seasons turned and the war raged on, she would have something else to hide, something far more precious, far more vulnerable, conceived in the stolen moments in the orchard, a living secret that would bind her forever to this quiet corner of Lincolnshire and to the man who carried the scars of Dunkirk.

# Chapter Three

Sophie hadn't been able to sleep properly since she found the letters. For three nights, the bundle of brittle paper, tied with its faded rust-red ribbon, had remained untouched on the bedside table in the small upstairs room. It was a tangible presence, a silent accusation, or perhaps an invitation, she couldn't yet discern which. The very thought of opening another filled her with a strange blend of reverence and unease. It was like finding someone's private diary, a raw, unfiltered chronicle of a soul, and knowing, with a deep certainty, that you had stumbled upon something profoundly sacred, something not meant for your eyes. Yet, despite this moral compunction, the temptation gnawed at her, a relentless, quiet itch under her skin. The words from the first letter echoed in her mind, fragments of Elsie's passion whispering in the quiet of the cottage, filling the silence that had so recently felt empty.

On the third morning, she woke early, not to the blare of an alarm or the distant rumble of London traffic, but to the delicate, almost musical sound of frost crackling at the windowpane. It was a sound both fragile and insistent, pulling her from the shallow depths of her restless sleep. The cold had seeped through the ancient glass, chilling the air around her face. She threw on her thickest wool coat, the one that smelled faintly of damp woodsmoke from the previous night's fire, and pulled on her worn leather boots. She needed air, needed to move, to shake off the unsettling quiet of the cottage and the even more unsettling whispers of Elsie's past.

Stepping outside, the world was transformed. The orchard, which had seemed skeletal and sombre just days before, was now rimmed with white, each twisted branch delicate and glittering in the early, nascent light. The frost had spun a fine, ephemeral lace over every twig and gnarled limb, turning the ancient trees into sculptures of ice and silver. Her breath plumed in the cold air, rising in soft clouds before dissipating into the vast stillness. She walked slowly, deliberately, between the trees, her boots crunching softly on the frozen ground, the sound sharp and clear in the profound quiet. She traced a path through the familiar lines of apple trees, the sensation of the rough bark beneath her gloved fingertips a grounding presence. She continued deeper into the orchard, following an instinct she couldn't name, until she reached the low stone wall at the very edge of the property, the crumbling boundary between Elsie's world and the wider, unknown fields beyond.

She sat there, letting the cold bite at her cheeks, a welcome sensation that brought her sharply into the present moment. Her gaze swept across the fields beyond the wall, a vast expanse of muted greens and browns stretching towards a distant, hazy horizon. A hare, a sudden blur of movement, darted from a hedgerow, its ears flattened against its back, and disappeared with astonishing speed into the distant, featureless landscape. Everything here felt so profoundly far removed from her old life. London, with its ceaseless noise and frantic hurry, the endless rush of commuters, the hollow, performative chatter of marketing meetings, the constant, low-level thrum of ambition and anxiety. Even the ache of her divorce, though still a tender bruise on her soul, felt somehow diminished, less immediate in this vast, indifferent landscape. Even now, weeks on, her mind still had a cruel tendency to replay the last argument with Daniel on an endless loop: the raised voices, the sudden, terrible quiet that descended, the sharp, final sound of the slammed door. And then, the crushing silence that followed, profound and irreversible. Daniel hadn't come after her. He hadn't called out her name. And a bitter voice in the back of her mind, a voice that sounded remarkably like her own, whispered that maybe he never really meant to.

The letters had opened something in her, a door she hadn't known was there. Not just simple curiosity, though that was certainly present, but a strange, aching kind of yearning. There was a softness to the words, a raw vulnerability that felt utterly alien in a world defined by superficial connections, by the curated facades of dating apps, and by the relentless pressure for performative happiness. Elsie's words were unpolished, unadorned, yet they pulsed with a profound, undeniable emotion. Whoever Elsie had been, whatever her life had contained, one thing was clear: she had loved this Thomas deeply, passionately, with a fierce devotion that poured off the page, saturating every line, every carefully chosen word.

Sophie thought about what it truly meant to love someone like that. To carry someone so profoundly within your heart, to articulate that love so vividly in words, even when they were gone, perhaps irrevocably. She had once thought, truly believed, that she loved Daniel. But not like this. Not with this kind of ache, this boundless devotion that permeated Elsie's every syllable. Her own love had been a more pragmatic, less volatile emotion, built on shared lives and common goals, not on the raw, open vulnerability that pulsed from Elsie's hidden confessions. It made her question everything she thought she knew about love, about commitment, about the silent depths of human connection.

Sophie stood, brushing frost from the cold, hard stone of the wall. The chill lingered on her fingertips, a reminder of the sharp, bracing reality of the morning. She would go into town today. Not just to wander, but with a purpose. She would try to learn more about Elsie, about Thomas, about the life that had unfolded in this quiet, unassuming place during a time of global turmoil. There was a local history archive in the village hall, according to the slightly crumpled leaflet she'd found in the welcome pack from the solicitor – a small, faded piece of paper that seemed almost comically out of place amidst the weight of Elsie's secrets. Maybe they'd have records. Maybe, just maybe, someone there would even remember Elsie, or at least the echoes of her story. The thought filled her with a tentative sense of hope, a direction she hadn't possessed in months.

The Village and its Whispers

The village of Fairfield was small, even by rural standards, its centre little more than a handful of shops – a tiny butcher, a bakery whose window displayed sturdy loaves of bread, a general store that seemed to sell everything from nails to teacups. Dominating the quiet main street was a post office, its red pillar box a familiar splash of colour, and a pub with a crooked chimney that leaned precariously against the winter sky, its chalkboard sign cheerfully advertising "Steak Pie & Real Ale." The village hall stood squarely beside the ancient, grey stone church, its own stone façade lined with thick, verdant ivy that seemed to cling to the past with tenacity. A light drizzle had started to fall as Sophie pulled up and parked her car outside the pub, the fine mist blurring the edges of the quaint scene. She wrapped her scarf tighter around her neck, pulling it up to shield her chin from the damp chill, and headed across the street, her boots splashing softly in the growing puddles.

Inside the village hall, the warmth was an immediate, palpable relief, a comforting blanket after the cold dampness outside. The air was rich with the scent of old paper, the faint tang of wood polish, and a surprising, pleasant hint of lemon cleaner. It was the smell of history, carefully preserved and quietly attended to. A woman in her sixties sat at a large wooden desk behind a glass counter, her silver hair neatly pulled back, her reading glasses perched on the end of her nose. She was meticulously cataloguing parish records, her movements economical and precise, the ease of someone who'd been doing this work for decades evident in every gesture. She looked up as Sophie approached, her eyes, though framed by sensible spectacles, held a keen, intelligent spark.

"Excuse me," Sophie said, her voice a little hesitant in the quiet space. "I was wondering if you have any local history archives?"

The woman looked up fully, a welcoming smile crinkling the corners of her eyes. "We do, indeed, dear. Quite a collection for a small village like ours. War records, family trees, even old council maps. All sorts of bits and bobs from bygone days." She gestured vaguely to shelves crammed with bound ledgers and filing cabinets. "Looking for something in particular?"

Sophie hesitated for a moment, gathering her thoughts, the story of the letters feeling almost too intimate to share with a stranger. But the woman's kind face, her warm, unhurried demeanour, encouraged her. She took a breath and nodded. "Yes, I think so. I recently inherited a cottage just outside the village. It belonged to my great-aunt, Elsie Hale. I found some letters—old ones. From the war." She watched for a reaction, a flicker of understanding.

Recognition, immediate and distinct, flickered in the woman's eyes, deepening the crinkles around them. A small smile, almost knowing, played on her lips. "Elsie Hale," she repeated, the name spoken with a gentle familiarity. "Lived in Orchard Cottage, didn't she? The one with the rather charming, if somewhat unruly, apple trees at the back?"

"Yes, that's the one," Sophie confirmed, a surprising rush of warmth blooming in her chest. Someone remembered Elsie. Someone knew her.

"Ah, Elsie," the woman mused, her gaze drifting for a moment, as if recalling distant memories. "She kept to herself mostly, in her later years, a bit of a recluse, some might say. But my mum used to say she was a real firebrand in her youth. Full of spirit, even a little rebellious, for a country girl. Something happened to her during the war, though, that much was clear. No one ever spoke about it directly, mind you, but there were whispers. My gran, bless her soul, used to say Elsie stopped going to dances after 1942. Just vanished into herself, she said. Lost her sparkle, as it were." The woman's voice carried a hint of affectionate sorrow, a testament to Elsie's impact, even in her later reticence.

Sophie felt her chest tighten, a sharp pang of empathy for this vibrant young woman who had apparently been dulled by the harsh hand of wartime. "Do you know if she had any children?" she asked, the question tumbling out before she could reconsider. It was a leap, a direct line from the letters and the implied love, but she had to ask. The woman's earlier caution about "secrets" lingered in her mind.

"Not that anyone knew of," the woman said carefully, her gaze meeting Sophie's, direct and understanding. "Not officially, anyway. But back then, dear, secrets were easier to keep. Especially for women. Especially when the war stirred everything up and sent folks far from home. Lives got complicated, fortunes shifted. Things that wouldn't have been tolerated before, well, they sometimes found a way to exist in the shadows." She sighed, a soft, wistful sound. "The war changed everyone, you see. And sometimes, the hardest battles weren't on the front lines, but right here, in people's hearts."

She stood then, a decisive movement, and gestured for Sophie to follow her towards a row of heavy, grey filing cabinets. "Come on, then. You might find more than you expect. Elsie was a local, even if she did come from a bit further afield initially. Her story's probably woven into these very pages."

She led Sophie to a specific cabinet, its metal cold under her touch, and with a practiced hand, pulled out a stack of faded, brittle documents: local census sheets, neatly bound; service records, typed and precise; and a few yellowing newspaper clippings. "You might try looking under wartime births, if you're thinking about children. Or evacuation records – sometimes families were separated, and children came here. We've also got a few personal accounts from that time—some of the Land Girls kept journals or wrote memoirs after the war. Fascinating reading, some of them. I'll dig out what I can while you start here." She gave Elsie a reassuring smile before disappearing into a back room, leaving Sophie surrounded by the quiet weight of history.

Threads of the Past

Sophie spent the next three hours sifting through dusty folders, her fingers growing smudged with the fine powder of decaying paper. The silence of the archive was broken only by the rustle of turning pages and the distant sound of rain pattering against the window. She examined grainy photographs, read clipped, formal reports, and tried to piece together the fragmented lives of people she had never known. She found a photograph taken in 1942, a group of Land Girls lined up outside a barn, their faces solemn yet determined, their uniforms practical and mud-stained. One of them— dark-haired, poised, her mouth set in a serious line, unsmiling—was unmistakably Elsie. Her eyes, even in the faded black and white, held that same intensity Sophie had seen in the portrait at the cottage. Elsie seemed almost to radiate a quiet strength, a defiance that contradicted the woman ~~Margaret~~ Marjorie described as having "lost her sparkle."

There was no direct mention of a Thomas Ashford. The name didn't appear in any local censuses, nor in the lists of men who had returned to the village from service. It was as if he were a ghost, a figment of Elsie's passionate wartime imagination. For a moment, a wave of disappointment washed over Sophie. Had she romanticised Elsie's story? Was this Thomas merely a creation of a lonely woman's longing?

But then, in a heavy folder specifically labelled "Local Military Placements, 1940-1941," amidst lists of convalescing soldiers and temporarily reassigned personnel, a familiar name suddenly jumped out at her, stark and undeniable in the neat, typed roster.

Private T. Ashford — Temporary leave, non-combat recovery assignment. Ravenswick Farm area.

She stared at it, the blood rushing to her ears, a triumphant surge of adrenaline making her hands tremble slightly. He had been real. This wasn't a romanticised invention, a fleeting wartime fiction conjured from loneliness and longing. He had lived, served, and passed through this very place, leaving a trace, however small, in the bureaucratic records of the war. Just like Elsie. The weight of his reality, now confirmed, made the letters pulsate with renewed life, their words suddenly imbued with an even deeper significance.

The archive woman returned a few minutes later, carrying a weathered journal bound in cracked leather, its pages thick and discoloured with age. "Here you go, dear," she said, her voice a soft murmur. "This belonged to one of the local farmers' daughters, a girl named Betty who kept a thorough record of daily life on the farm. She mentions Elsie a few times, mostly in passing, but it paints a picture of what she was like to others. Says she was always wandering into the orchard with some soldier lad. Quiet type, Betty called him. Always writing letters, our Elsie. Never posting them, though, which Betty thought was a bit odd." The woman smiled, a conspiratorial glint in her eye. "Seemed to hint at a secret romance, even back then."

Sophie smiled back, a genuine, unforced smile that reached her eyes. "That sounds like her," she murmured, thinking of the hidden bundle, the words never meant for outward journey. It was a poignant detail, confirming Elsie's solitary devotion, her need to keep this love contained, protected.

She left the hall with a folder of scanned records – the photograph of Elsie among the Land Girls, the typed roster confirming Thomas Ashford's presence – all safely tucked into her notebook. Rain had started in earnest now, a steady downpour that drummed on the roof of her car and speckled her windscreen as she drove back through the winding country roads. The wipers moved rhythmically, clearing small arcs of visibility, but her mind was elsewhere, lost in the unfolding narrative of Elsie's past.

Reopening the Past
That evening, back in the quiet sanctuary of the cottage, the fire she had carefully built earlier now cast a warm, flickering glow across the living room. The air was filled with the comforting scent of woodsmoke and damp earth. Sophie sat cross-legged on the rug in front of the hearth, the letters once again spread out before her, no longer a forbidden discovery, but an urgent invitation. The confirmation from the archive, the tangible proof of Thomas's existence, had dissolved her earlier hesitation. She felt a profound sense of permission, almost an obligation, to bear witness to Elsie's story.

She selected the second one from the bundle, her fingers tracing the neat, elegant script. It was dated June 1941, a time when spring was surely bursting into full bloom in Lincolnshire. She unfolded it carefully, savouring the anticipation.

"My Dearest Thomas," she read aloud, her voice soft, tentative at first, then growing stronger, as if channeling Elsie herself. The words filled the small room, tangible and resonant. "The orchard is green now. You wouldn't recognise it. The apples are coming in early this year, Margaret says. She thinks the soil is good luck. I like to think it's you, Thomas. That you left some part of yourself behind when you walked among these trees, a promise whispered to the roots. I miss you terribly. Every day is longer without you, every chore heavier. They say you'll be back before the first frost. I count the days, each one a tiny victory against the waiting. I trace your name in the dust on my windowsill when no one is looking."

Sophie read it aloud again, slowly, letting each word resonate within her. Her voice felt foreign in the profound quiet, like she was borrowing someone else's story, inhabiting a life not her own. And yet, something in it anchored her, pulled her deeper into Elsie's world, making the boundaries between past and present blur. The image of Elsie, alone in her cottage, tracing Thomas's name, was a powerful one, conveying a loneliness and longing that transcended time.

She opened another letter, this one from late July. The paper was thinner, almost translucent, as if Elsie had used the last scrap she could find.

"The sky turned dark this morning," Elsie had written, her hand perhaps more hurried, the words imbued with a subtle anxiety. "Not with rain, but with silence. It pressed against the windows like a held breath, a great, invisible weight. The air was heavy, still. I wonder where you are, Thomas. If you saw the same oppressive sky, if you felt the same profound silence. If you thought of me, even for a moment, as I thought of you. Do you ever feel this quiet, this vastness, or is the war too loud for anything else?"

Sophie felt tears prick at the corners of her eyes, a warm, unexpected wetness. There was something so exquisitely intimate in Elsie's words. Not dramatic in a theatrical sense. Not overly poetic or flowery. Just real. Honest. Unvarnished.

The raw, open kind of love that Sophie realised, with a pang of bittersweet recognition, she had never dared to express, never truly experienced herself. Her own relationships had been built on careful boundaries, on polite unspoken rules, on a fear of exposing too much, of being too vulnerable. Elsie's love, however, was a force of nature, untamed and unashamed. It made Sophie ache for something she hadn't known she was missing.

She folded the letters carefully, reverently, returning them to their brittle envelopes. Then, on a powerful, undeniable impulse, she crossed to the small wooden writing desk by the window—the one that had been covered in a thick layer of dust until she had wiped it clean just yesterday. She opened her old journal, the one she had retrieved from her box of keepsakes, the one filled with abandoned stories and half-formed thoughts.

She picked up her pen, its familiar weight comforting in her hand, and began to write, the words flowing with an ease she hadn't felt in years.

Today I found her. Not just her letters. Not just the remnants of her life in this quiet cottage. I found her voice. Her vibrant, yearning heart. Her orchard, now a place of whispered secrets. Her sorrow, deep and unyielding. I don't know what this is yet, this unfolding story, this connection I feel. But it feels like the start of something. Something profound. Something true.

She paused, the pen hovering over the page, her gaze drifting to the flickering fire. Then, a new wave of thought propelled her hand forward, the words pouring out, raw and honest.

Daniel never looked at me the way she wrote about him. Maybe that's unfair. Maybe the memory of love is always sweeter, more profound, when seen through the lens of history. Or maybe I'm only seeing it now, truly understanding the depth of that kind of devotion, because I finally have the quiet to listen. The incessant noise of my old life, the endless distractions, they never allowed for this kind of introspection. This kind of stillness. I wonder what I would write if I truly thought no one would ever read it. What secrets would emerge? What desires? What fears? Maybe I'll try. Maybe that's where I start. By writing only for myself, as Elsie wrote only for Thomas, and for the silence between the floorboards.

She closed the book gently, the soft thud of the cover echoing slightly in the quiet room. She stared into the dancing flames, the heat a comforting presence against the lingering chill of the cottage. The air no longer felt empty, but alive with the echoes of Elsie's voice, the quiet hum of history, and the nascent stirrings of her own renewed spirit.

It was the first thing she'd written in years, a tentative step onto a new path.

But it wouldn't be the last.

# Chapter Four

Lincolnshire, Late Summer 1941

The letter arrived on a Wednesday. It appeared with an almost deceptive simplicity, a thin, unassuming rectangle of paper slipped halfway through the letterbox of Elsie's cottage door, its corners softened and slightly dog-eared from its journey, its colour a stark white against the dark wood. Elsie had just returned from the fields, her body a symphony of aches, muscles protesting with every movement. Mud, thick and clinging, was caked up her shins, reaching almost to her knees, and her arms throbbed from a morning spent in the relentless, repetitive labour of lifting crates of potatoes, their earthy scent clinging to her clothes and skin. For weeks, the sky had been a monotonous canvas of grey, a relentless shroud that seemed to dampen even the spirit. But today, finally, the sun had broken through, painting the late summer landscape in hues of gold and warmth. The orchard, once skeletal and barren, now buzzed with the lazy hum of insects, a symphony of bees and flies drawn to the sweet, heavy scent of fermenting windfall apples that lay scattered across the grass like forgotten jewels.

She pulled off her heavy, mud-caked boots at the cottage door, the familiar ritual of shedding the outside world. As she straightened, she saw it—the letter. Her heart, already beating steadily from exertion, gave a sudden, sharp lurch. The white envelope seemed to glow in the dim light of the hallway. She recognized the handwriting instantly, a familiar slant that she had only seen on the addresses of the few letters she received, but which had etched itself onto her memory. It was Thomas's script, unmistakable and utterly unexpected.

Inside the small, quiet sanctuary of her cottage, with hands that trembled despite her best efforts to steady them, she tore it open. The paper, crisp and slightly rough, ripped with a sound that seemed disproportionately loud in the stillness.

"Elsie," the letter began, his familiar, understated tone already present in the concise words. "Orders have come. I leave on Saturday."

Elsie's breath caught in her throat. She knew this was coming. Every man was needed, every able body thrown into the insatiable maw of the war. But knowing something intellectually and having it delivered with such stark finality were two entirely different experiences.

"I tried to delay. Doctor says I'm fit enough to return and they need every man they can get. I'm told we'll ship out to the south coast first, then France again—maybe farther."

France again. The words echoed with the chilling weight of his past. Dunkirk. Shrapnel. The quiet suffering she had glimpsed in his eyes. He was being sent back to the heart of it, to the brutal, unpredictable theatre of war. A cold knot formed in the pit of her stomach.

"Meet me tomorrow evening. The orchard, near the stone wall. Just after sunset."

The orchard. Their place. The sanctuary where their fragile, blossoming connection had taken root. The promise of one last meeting, a desperate, final chance.

"I'll wait for you."

A single, potent sentence, a promise, a plea.

"Yours,"

And then, his name, simple and profound. "Thomas."

She read it twice. Then a third time, her eyes tracing each word, as if by sheer concentration she could alter their meaning, soften their impact. Her legs felt suddenly weak, a strange, liquid sensation spreading through her limbs. She sank onto the small wooden stool by the door, the letter still clutched in her hand. It wasn't unexpected—she had known, in the abstract way of wartime, that this day would eventually come—but now that it had, the finality of it pressed against her chest like a physical weight, a suffocating burden she couldn't lift, couldn't shrug off. The silence of the cottage, once a comfort, now felt oppressive, amplifying the frantic thud of her own heart.

That evening, she lay in bed, staring unseeing at the darkened ceiling. She didn't light the fire. The late summer air was warm, unusually so for Lincolnshire, but she welcomed the subtle chill that settled over her skin. She wanted silence, a stark absence of sound that might somehow allow her to hear her own chaotic thoughts. She thought of the orchard, the place where they had shared quiet words and even quieter glances. She replayed their last conversation, the way his eyes had searched hers, a silent question passing between them, without saying what they both knew was coming. The unspoken promise that hung in the air, a delicate thread they had both been too afraid to grasp fully.

She had begun writing him a letter that afternoon, a desperate attempt to capture all the words she hadn't said, all the feelings she had bottled up. Her pen had flown across the page, a torrent of emotion. Then she had stopped. The words felt hollow, inadequate, insignificant in the face of this kind of goodbye. How could mere ink on paper convey the overwhelming reality of his imminent departure, the gnawing fear that he might never return?

The Last Sunset
The next day passed in a disorienting daze. Elsie moved through her farm chores like a somnambulist, her body performing the familiar tasks while her mind was utterly elsewhere, caught in a swirling vortex of fear and longing. She worked the fields, her hands automatically sorting potatoes, feeding the chickens, but her eyes saw only blurred shapes, her ears heard only a muffled hum. Margaret said nothing, her no-nonsense efficiency somehow softened by a silent understanding. Perhaps she sensed something in Elsie's quietness, a change in her usual resolute demeanour. Perhaps she had seen this scene play out too many times before.

By sunset, the sky a vast canvas painted in muted golds, fading to soft lavenders and bruised purples, Elsie had changed into her cleanest clothes—a soft, worn blue blouse that accentuated the colour of her eyes, and a practical brown wool skirt. They were her best, simple yet carefully chosen, an unspoken tribute to the significance of the meeting. Her hands were scrubbed raw, the ingrained dirt of the fields finally banished, her nails neatly trimmed. Her dark hair, usually escaping in wisps around her face, was tied neatly behind her ears, a desperate attempt at composure.

She walked to the orchard as the last sliver of sun slid behind the trees, casting long, distorted shadows that stretched across the land like reaching fingers. The air, still warm from the day, now carried the faint scent of damp earth and late-blooming wildflowers. The silence of the orchard felt different tonight; it was no longer merely peaceful, but charged with a heavy, anticipatory stillness, as if the very trees held their breath alongside her.

Thomas was already there. He stood with his back to her, a solitary silhouette against the fading light, his arms folded across his chest as he stared across the open field beyond the low stone wall. His posture was rigid, tense. She paused at the edge of the trees, hidden by the deepening shadows, watching him for a moment. The uniform sat heavily on his frame now. Not new anymore, not crisp and uncreased like the day he had arrived. It was worn in, weighted, imbued with the dust of roads and the unspoken stories of men marching, the burden of a war that claimed not just lives, but souls. He seemed older, the quiet intensity in his eyes deepened by something she couldn't quite decipher.

He turned at the soft sound of her footsteps, his movements swift and fluid despite the implied weight of his uniform. His eyes, dark and fathomless in the twilight, met hers.

"You came," he said, his voice low, a quiet exhalation of relief.

"Of course I did," she replied, the words a gentle rebuke, a statement of unshakeable certainty. There was nowhere else she could be.

They stood in silence for a long, stretched beat, the wind rustling through the leaves of the ancient trees around them, a mournful whisper. The air thrummed with unspoken words, with the crushing weight of their imminent parting.

"I wish it didn't have to be this way," he said quietly, his voice rough with emotion, his gaze fixed on the ground between them.

"So do I," she replied, her voice barely a whisper, the simple words carrying the immense weight of shared sorrow.

He looked up then, his dark eyes searching hers, a vulnerability she hadn't seen before clouding their depths. "I don't want to leave anything unsaid."

Elsie felt a surge of courage, a desperate defiance against the inevitability of their situation. She stepped closer, closing the small distance between them. "Then don't," she urged, her hand reaching out, almost touching his arm, then hesitating.

He reached into the deep pocket of his greatcoat and pulled out a small piece of folded fabric. It was a handkerchief, soft and worn, laundered countless times, its edges frayed. Embroidered delicately in one corner, in a faded blue thread, were the initials "T.A." His own. He held it out to her, his hand steady despite the tremor in his voice. "It's not much. It's just... a bit of me. But it's yours if you want it."

She took it, her fingers brushing against his, the worn fabric surprisingly soft against her palm. A small, genuine smile touched her lips, a fragile blossom in the face of sorrow. "Then you should have something too. Wait."

She reached into the inner pocket of her coat, a place she rarely used, and pulled out a delicate silver locket on a thin, almost invisible chain. It was her grandmother's, passed down to her. Inside, carefully folded and protected, was a small photo of her, taken the previous spring by a street photographer in London—her only one, a rare moment of captured youth and innocence. "It's not much either," she said, her voice soft, pressing it into his hand, closing his fingers around it gently. "But keep it close. Keep it safe. And if you ever feel alone... look at it and remember what's waiting for you. Remember me."

He opened the locket, his thumb tracing the small, sepia image of her face. A soft, tender smile spread across his lips, transforming his usually serious expression. "I will," he murmured, his gaze lifting to meet hers, holding hers with an intense, unspoken promise. "Every day. Every moment." His voice dropped, losing its already fragile composure, becoming a raw whisper. "Elsie, if I don't come back—"

"Don't," she said, her voice catching, the word sharp, desperate. She couldn't bear it, not now, not when they had so little time. "Don't talk like that. You will come back."

He reached for her hands then, his fingers intertwining with hers, holding them tightly, as if he could somehow impart his strength, his resolve. "Then let me say this instead. I've never felt like this before. Not in all my life. Not with anyone. You make everything quiet inside my head, Elsie. All the noise, all the fear, it just... stops. You make me feel like I belong somewhere. Like I have a home."

Tears welled in Elsie's eyes, hot and sudden, blurring his face. "You do belong," she whispered, her voice choked with emotion. "You belong. With me. Here. Always."

He leaned forward then, slowly, deliberately, and kissed her. It wasn't rushed or stolen, not a hurried peck of a goodbye. It was deep, certain, and slow, a profound connection that spoke volumes more than any words. Her hands found the sides of his face, her thumbs tracing the strong lines of his jaw, his slightly rough skin. His arms wrapped around her, pulling her close, anchoring them both together in a desperate, timeless embrace. The scent of him – clean wool, faint metal, and something uniquely his, something warm and comforting – filled her senses. They held each other there for a long, immeasurable time, until the last vestiges of the sun faded from gold to deep, bruised twilight.

"Stay a little longer," she whispered, her voice muffled against his shoulder, a plea born of desperate hope.

He nodded, pressing his face into her hair. "As long as I can. Every precious second."

A Shared Night, A Secret Promise
They returned to the cottage, walking quietly, their fingers entwined, a silent pact against the world. Inside, the firelight cast soft, dancing shadows on the walls, making the small room feel intimate and warm. It was the first time Thomas had been inside her cottage, the first time he had truly stepped into her solitary world. He looked around, his gaze taking in the simple furnishings, the flickering flames, the quiet domesticity. He squeezed her hand, a silent acknowledgement of the significance of this step.

There were no words. They didn't need them. Everything that needed to be said was conveyed in the language of touch, of breath, of shared silence. Clothes were unbuttoned gently, hesitantly, with a reverence that elevated the act beyond mere physical desire. Each touch was slow, deliberate, exploring, a tender revelation. They moved together like they had waited a hundred years for this moment, like two pieces of a puzzle finally clicking into place. It wasn't hurried or desperate, though the urgency of his departure hung heavy in the air. It was filled with everything they hadn't said, every suppressed emotion, every unspoken hope, every whispered dream. It was a communion of souls, a fleeting eternity against the backdrop of a brutal war.

Afterwards, they lay together beneath the worn, familiar blankets, their skin warm from the fire and the shared intimacy, their hearts thudding quietly in time, a soft, reassuring rhythm in the stillness of the night. The scent of him, of her, of their shared space, was a profound comfort.

He kissed her shoulder, a light, tender brush of his lips against her skin. "If I could stay forever, Elsie," he murmured, his voice thick with emotion, "I would."

She looked at him, her eyes shining in the dim light, wet with unshed tears. Her fingers traced the line of his jaw, the gentle curve of his ear. "Then come back," she whispered, the words a desperate, fervent prayer. "Come back to me."

For a timeless moment, the world outside the cottage ceased to exist. The orchard around them, the war that raged across continents, the chilling uncertainty of what was coming—all of it dissolved into that single, shared moment of profound connection. There was only them, and the fragile, precious bubble of their love.

When they finally, reluctantly, pulled apart, his forehead rested against hers, their breaths mingling, their eyes closed.

"Promise me something," he said, his voice husky, almost a plea.

"Anything," she replied instantly, without hesitation.

"Keep writing," he urged, his voice low, firm. "Even if I can't write back. Leave them where we said. In the cottage. In the earth. They'll be waiting. A message for when I return. A way for me to find you."

She nodded, tears streaming down her face now, unable to speak, her throat tight with emotion. The promise was sacred, a lifeline thrown across an abyss.

He stepped back, and she wanted to pull him close again, to cling to him, to defy the inevitable, but she let him go. She watched him move towards the door, then turn, his dark eyes finding hers one last time.

"I'll come back to you," he vowed, his voice clear, resolute, ringing with conviction. "One way or another."

Then he was gone, a shadow disappearing into the pre-dawn grey, leaving only the lingering warmth of his presence, the echo of his words, and the profound ache of his absence.

Waiting and Whispers
A week had passed. A week that felt like an eternity, each day a slow, measured tick of the clock of absence. The mornings came quietly, each one a little colder than the last, drawing ever closer to the first frost that Thomas had mentioned. Elsie kept herself busy on the farm, throwing herself into the relentless physical labour, not trusting her hands to be idle,

not trusting her mind to be unoccupied. The work was a brutal balm, a physical exhaustion that dulled the sharper edges of her grief. She hadn't heard anything since Thomas left, no news, no message, and the silence pressed heavy on her chest, a constant, suffocating weight. Every distant aeroplane, every unexpected knock at the door, sent a jolt of anxious hope through her, only to be quickly dashed.

Then, on a mist-soaked morning, as the sun struggled to burn through the clinging, ethereal fog that veiled the fields, a letter arrived. It was pushed through her letterbox with a soft rustle, a sound that made her heart leap into her throat.

The envelope was crumpled and smudged, the paper softened, the ink faded from rain or sweat or time, or perhaps all three. It bore the marks of a long, arduous journey through a war-torn landscape. But it was unmistakably his. The sight of his familiar, strong script on the outside sent a wave of relief and fear washing over her in equal measure.

She tore it open, her fingers fumbling with the damp paper.

"Elsie," it began, his voice, though written, clear in her mind. "Only a moment to write. We've moved three times in five days. Always moving. Always pushing forward. The days blur. I still carry the locket you gave me. It's foolish, I suppose, a small bit of vanity in this brutal landscape, but it helps. It reminds me what quiet feels like, what hope tastes like. It keeps you close."

A profound wave of tenderness washed over Elsie. He was safe. He was thinking of her. The locket, a tiny piece of her, was with him.

"I read your letters when I can. When they reach me. Sometimes it's days, sometimes weeks. Sometimes they disappear. We're moving more often now, faster than the mail can keep up. I don't know how many will make it through anymore, so maybe it's safer to leave them where we said. In the cottage. In our place. I'll look for them when I come home. Keep writing, Elsie. Don't stop. They are a lifeline. They are a promise."

"Always,
Thomas"

It was brief. Terribly brief. But it was everything. It was a connection across the vast, terrifying distance. It was confirmation of their shared secret, their hidden pact. It was a promise.

She read it three times, letting each word sink deep into her soul, memorizing its cadence, its meaning. Then, with an almost sacred gesture, she folded it carefully and slipped it into the inner lining of her coat, pressing it against her heart, as if its physical proximity could offer protection, could keep him close.

That night, she lit a single candle on her small table, its flame a beacon in the encroaching darkness. She took out her notebook, the blank page a silent invitation.

"My Dearest Thomas," she wrote, her pen moving with a newfound clarity, a desperate urgency. "I kept my promise. I met you at sunset, and the orchard stood still around us, a silent witness to our farewell. If this letter never finds its way into your hands, lost somewhere in the chaos of battle, I hope it finds its way into the air around you. I hope it brushes past you when the wind shifts, carrying a whisper of my love, or lands softly on your shoulder as you rest, a gentle reminder that you are not forgotten. You took something with you when you left—not just my heart, which you certainly carry, but the very breath in my lungs, the solid soil beneath my feet, the warmth in my skin. All of me, bound to you."

She paused, looking at the words, willing them to travel across the sea, to reach him, to find him.

"I'll write again soon. Every day. Every day you are gone, a new word, a new thought, a new prayer will be waiting for you here. In our cottage. In our orchard."

"Come back to me. Always."

She folded the letter, a delicate, fragile hope contained within its creases, and tied it with a fresh length of ribbon, a brighter red than the faded one she'd found. With a quiet, determined resolve, she placed it under the same loose floorboard in her bedroom, a secret message awaiting its recipient, a lifeline woven from words and unwavering love.

The night creaked around her, the old cottage settling into its own unique rhythm of sighs and groans. The orchard stood in silence outside, a sentinel of memory.

She waited for morning, and for the next letter she would write. And the next. And the next.

# Chapter Five

Sophie leaned back in the worn chair by the kitchen window, cradling a mug of tea gone cold. The ceramic felt smooth and heavy against her palms, its forgotten warmth a minor comfort in the grey light that permeated the room. The morning had slipped away in a relentless drizzle, a soft, insistent drumming against the windowpane and the ancient roof tiles. She hadn't noticed the passage of time, so completely lost was she in the unfolding narrative of Elsie's hidden life, until the clock in the hall chimed noon, its sonorous bongs echoing through the quiet cottage like a gentle reprimand. Her laptop was open in front of her, its screen a bright, unblemished rectangle, but she hadn't typed anything yet. The cursor blinked expectantly, a tiny, impatient pulse against the vast white space.

Three more letters had surfaced that week. Each time she pried up the loose floorboard in Elsie's bedroom, her heart raced with a familiar mix of reverence and unease, a curious blend of anticipation and apprehension. The wood groaned softly under her touch, releasing a puff of fine, ancient dust that danced in the slivers of light. She'd read each one carefully, meticulously, as though they might disintegrate under her gaze, their fragile paper dissolving into memory. The ink had faded to a sepia whisper, softening the starkness of Elsie's careful script, but the raw, unbridled emotion hadn't dimmed in the slightest. It was as vibrant and urgent as the day it was penned, resonating across the decades. The last letter she'd read had been dated September 1941, coinciding chillingly with Thomas's return to active service.

Elsie's handwriting, usually so precise and controlled, had grown tighter, more uncertain in these later letters. The sentences carried a palpable weight they hadn't possessed before, like Elsie was trying desperately to hold something together that was beginning, inexorably, to slip through her fingers. The tone had shifted, subtly but distinctly, from hopeful longing to a more fragile, anxious yearning. Sophie hadn't reached the very end of the hidden bundle yet, but she could feel it approaching, a sombre inevitability, like reaching the final, devastating chapter of a cherished book. A sense of dread mingled with her insatiable curiosity.

She took a slow, cold sip of her tea, the bitter liquid doing little to chase away the chill that had settled deep within her. She opened her journal, the one she'd started writing in again, and the blank page stared back, demanding words.

"Today I read a letter where Elsie mentioned the sound of church bells and how, even amidst the war, they made her feel like hope was still possible. A steady, ringing promise through the chaos."

She paused, her fingers hovering over the keyboard, the memory of Elsie's careful words echoing in her mind. Then, a thought, stark and perhaps a little cynical, formed. She typed, the soft click of the keys a rhythmic counterpoint to the quiet drizzle outside:

"I haven't heard a church bell in years, not without thinking of funerals. Not without the mournful toll that marks an ending. Maybe we've forgotten how to listen for hope. Maybe the incessant noise of our modern lives, the constant updates and anxieties, has deafened us to quieter forms of reassurance. Or maybe we've simply stopped believing in the possibility of it."

She saved the document, the small whir of the laptop's hard drive a momentary disruption in the cottage's profound quiet, and shut the lid with a soft click. The thoughts lingered, a challenging question about her own perception of the world.

Unearthing Thomas

That afternoon, driven by an urgent need for more answers, Sophie returned to the village hall. The light drizzle had intensified into a steady rain, blurring the quaint lines of Fairfield village. Marjorie, the archivist, greeted her with a small, knowing smile, as if expecting her, and a thicker stack of papers than Sophie had seen last time. Her eyes held a spark of gentle curiosity, an unspoken invitation to delve deeper.

"I pulled what I could find on Ashford, dear," Marjorie said, her voice soft, almost sympathetic. "There's not a lot, as you might expect with military records from that time. So many gaps. But it might help you piece things together. Might give you some clarity." She placed the folder gently on the counter, a silent acknowledgement of the sensitivity of the contents.

Sophie took the folder to the reading table, the one she'd used before, its polished surface reflecting the dim light from the window. She opened it gently, almost reverently, as if the papers within were fragile ancient artifacts.

Inside were a handful of official documents. There were crumpled ration card entries, mundane details of sustenance in a time of scarcity. A page from the local school registry, documenting a young Thomas Ashford's attendance, his birthdate and parents' names handwritten in faded ink. And then, the military references. Three terse, official entries that contained the stark, chilling trajectory of his service. One mentioned Private Thomas Ashford's medical furlough in 1940, confirming his injuries and recovery in the local area. Another, stark and unembellished, listed his return to active service by September 1941 – the very month Elsie's letters had begun to tighten, to carry their unspoken weight of fear. The final entry, a brief, almost dismissive notice in a regional military bulletin, stated, with chilling brevity, that his unit had been stationed near Caen by late October.

Nothing more.

No mention of his fate. No record of his return. No official recognition of his end. Just a stark, terrible silence. Sophie's heart sank, a heavy, leaden feeling settling in her chest. She turned the pages slowly, meticulously, her fingers tracing the faded type, hoping against hope for a mention of Elsie. A letter confirming their connection. A note from a comrade. A whisper of something, anything, that could fill the vast, terrifying void left by those two words: "Nothing more." But there was only blankness.

"Did anyone ever interview the Land Girls who worked in this area?" Sophie asked, desperate for another avenue, a human voice that might offer what the dry records could not. Her own voice sounded thin, almost strained, in the quiet of the archive.

Marjorie nodded, her gaze thoughtful. "A few, yes. We tried to gather their stories for posterity. Most have passed now, of course. Time takes its toll on us all." She paused, her finger tapping her lip. "But there's a woman still living out near Branton Hill—Beatrice Lane. She was part of the Women's Land Army, worked on a farm not far from Ravenswick. She was quite the chatterbox, I recall. Said she remembered a girl who 'kept to herself, always scribbling in notebooks and disappearing into the orchard.'" Marjorie's eyes twinkled with a knowing warmth. "Sound familiar, does it?"

Sophie's heart gave a hopeful flutter. It sounded exactly like Elsie. She scribbled the name down, the pen scratching furiously on the paper, the tangible act grounding her. Beatrice Lane. A living link to Elsie's past.

"Could I speak to her?" Sophie asked, her voice imbued with a newfound urgency. "Would she be willing?"

"You could certainly try, dear. She's in her nineties now, well into them, but sharp as a tack when she wants to be. Her memory might be a little patchy on the details, but the general gist is usually there. And she does love a good cup of tea and a visitor. I'll ring ahead if you like, let her know you're coming. Saves a wasted journey."

Sophie accepted gratefully, a fragile hope blossoming in her chest. Beatrice Lane. A witness. Someone who had seen Elsie, perhaps even seen Thomas, within the very landscape that now held their secrets.

The Witness
Driving out to Branton Hill felt like crossing into another world entirely. The familiar, low-lying fields around Fairfield gave way to a more undulating landscape, the hedgerows growing higher, thicker, forming dense, protective walls along the winding lanes. The fields themselves were open and wind-worn, stretching in vast, unbroken swathes under the perpetually grey sky. The drizzle continued, a fine, persistent mist that softened the edges of the distant trees

and blurred the horizon. Sophie followed a narrow, winding lane, barely wide enough for one car, until she reached a modest, neat white cottage. Its blue shutters, though faded, provided a cheerful contrast to the muted landscape, and a bird feeder swayed gently by the front door, attracting a flurry of small, grey birds. It was a place that exuded a quiet resilience, a sense of having weathered many seasons.

Beatrice Lane answered on the second knock, her movements slow but deliberate. She leaned heavily on a carved wooden cane, its polished surface worn smooth by years of use. Her eyes, though pale with age, were remarkably alert, keen, missing nothing. She peered at Sophie, her head cocked slightly to one side, a faint smile playing on her lips before Sophie could even utter a greeting.

"You're the girl asking about Elsie Hale," she said, her voice surprisingly strong, though raspy with age, cutting straight to the chase. There was no need for pleasantries, no beating around the bush.

"Yes," Sophie confirmed, a faint blush rising to her cheeks at being so immediately identified. "Yes, I am. I inherited her cottage. And... I've found some of her letters." She held her breath, waiting for a reaction.

Beatrice nodded slowly, a knowing glint in her pale eyes. She took a moment, her gaze seeming to measure Sophie, to weigh her intentions. Then, with a sigh that was more of contentment than weariness, she stepped aside, opening the door wider.

"Come in, dearie. Don't stand out in that miserable damp. But I'm warning you now," she added, her eyes twinkling with a flash of dry humour, "I'm not walking you through my life story unless there's proper tea involved. Strong, with milk and two sugars. And maybe a biscuit, if I've got any left."

An hour later, they sat in a quiet, surprisingly cosy room. The floral wallpaper, though cracked and faded in places, still retained a faint vibrancy, a ghostly echo of its original cheerful pattern. A low-burning gas fire hissed softly in the grate, casting a faint warmth that slowly began to thaw the chill in Sophie's bones. The air smelled of old lavender, dust, and something else – something resilient, something of long-lived life. Sophie nursed her own mug of tea, now hot and sweet, as she listened, truly listened, to Beatrice.

Beatrice talked about long mornings in the fields, the physical toll of farm work under the relentless demands of wartime. She spoke of blistered hands and broken tools, of shared cigarettes smuggled behind barns, of whispered songs sung to ward off the monotony. She described the camaraderie among the Land Girls, a bond forged in shared hardship, and the quiet pride they took in their essential work. She painted a vivid picture of a time both incredibly difficult and strangely fulfilling. Then, her voice softened, and she paused, stirring her tea slowly, her gaze distant, lost in memory.

"Elsie was different," Beatrice said, her voice dropping to a more reflective tone. "Not cold, mind you. Never cold. Just... private. More so than the rest of us. Always off in her own world, you might say. You'd see her staring out across the orchard, sometimes, like she was waiting for something to appear out of the trees, someone only she could see. She kept herself to herself, but you felt her presence, strong as stone."

Sophie leaned forward, her heart quickening. This was it. The direct link. "Do you remember anything about Thomas Ashford?" she asked, keeping her voice steady, despite the tremor of anticipation.

Beatrice looked down at her gnarled hands, tracing the lines on her palm, her expression unreadable for a long moment. A profound sadness, faint but unmistakable, settled over her features. "Ah, Thomas," she murmured, the name spoken with a tender resonance. "Tall lad. Dark hair. Always had a quiet way about him. Kind. Too kind for the uniform he wore, perhaps." Her eyes lifted to meet Sophie's, clear and direct. "They were close, Elsie and him. Everyone knew it. Not in a scandalous way, you understand, not the way some of the others carried on. Just... bound. You could feel it, the connection between them. A quiet understanding. Like two parts of the same whole."

A wave of emotion washed over Sophie, a bittersweet ache of recognition. This was the love in the letters, confirmed by a living witness. "Do you know what happened to him?" she asked, the words barely a whisper, dreading the answer, yet desperate for it.

Beatrice sighed, a long, weary sound. "Only what the papers said, dear. The official notices. Missing after an engagement in France. Late '41 or early '42, I think. Caen, was it? Something like that. Never came back. Just... vanished. Like so many others." Her voice held the quiet resignation of a generation that had seen too much loss.

Sophie sat quietly, the words heavy, crushing, echoing the silence of the official records. "Missing." A word that promised no closure, only an endless, agonizing question mark. She imagined Elsie, waiting, hoping, clinging to a promise that would never be fulfilled.

"She waited for him," Beatrice added, her gaze fixed on the dancing flames of the gas fire, her voice barely audible. "Always writing, always scribbling into those little notebooks of hers, filling them with words meant only for him. Said she had to finish the story, she told me once. Finish the story, whether anyone ever read it or not. Said it was her way of keeping him alive. Keeping him close."

Sophie's throat tightened, a lump forming that made it impossible to speak. Tears, hot and uncontrollable, welled in her eyes. "I am," she whispered, her voice raw, catching on the emotion. "I'm reading them. I'm finishing the story."

Beatrice gave a slow smile, a profound, gentle expression that softened the lines of age on her face. Her pale eyes, ancient and wise, held a deep understanding. "Then maybe that's enough," she said softly. "Maybe that's all anyone can ask for."

A Promise to the Past
Back at the cottage, the rain still drumming against the windowpanes, Sophie laid out the letters again on the worn kitchen table. The confirmation of Thomas's fate, the crushing finality of "missing," solidified a terrible truth. She was starting to understand, with a clarity that was both painful and deeply moving. These weren't just love letters, written in a surge of wartime passion. They were Elsie's lifeline. Her anchor in a world consumed by chaos. Her legacy. Her defiant truth spoken in silence, entrusted to the

earth beneath her feet. They were a monument to a love that transcended absence, a fierce refusal to let go.

She opened the next one, her fingers trembling slightly. It was dated November 1941, the bleak heart of autumn, just weeks after Thomas's unit had been near Caen. Elsie's script was indeed tighter, more desperate.

"My Dearest Thomas," Sophie read aloud, her voice now imbued with Elsie's sorrow, "The nights are longer now, vast, empty stretches of darkness. The orchard has lost its leaves, a stark skeleton against the indifferent sky, like everything else, stripped bare. I walked its edge today, feeling the biting wind, and saw a fox dart across your path, a swift, reddish blur against the muted earth. I imagine you out there, Thomas, walking the same desolate way, feeling the same cold, seeing the same empty sky. I hold your handkerchief every morning before I start the day, pressing its soft fabric to my cheek. It's worn now, softened from countless touches, faded from time, but it still smells faintly of you, a ghost of your presence. Sometimes I press it to my lips, and in those moments, I can almost convince myself that you're just beyond the orchard, about to step through the trees, a living, breathing miracle. The hope is a painful thing, a sharp, fragile shard in my heart."

She paused, her breath catching. The raw longing, the desperate, almost delusional hope, was palpable.

"I have to believe you'll come back to me. I simply have to. Without that belief, there is nothing. I cannot bear the thought."

"Please don't be a ghost."

Sophie set the letter down gently, as if it might shatter, tears stinging her eyes, blurring the page. The final line, so simple, so utterly devastating in its plea, ripped through her. Elsie had known. Deep down, she had known the truth, even as she fought it with every fibre of her being.

She reached for her journal again, the laptop still open beside her, its screen a silent witness. The need to write, to process this wave of grief for a woman and a love she had never known, was overwhelming.

"Elsie didn't stop writing, even when the world gave her every reason to. Even when hope seemed a cruel joke. Even when the man she loved was declared missing, probably lost forever to the brutal machinery of war. Maybe that's what true love is: a relentless act of faith against all odds. Or maybe it's simply what faith looks like, manifested in ink and paper, a quiet defiance in the face of despair."

She saved it, the soft click of the mouse a final punctuation mark.

Then she whispered to the empty room, to the quiet cottage, to the lingering spirit of Elsie that now felt so vividly present: "I won't stop either. I will see your story finished. For you. For Thomas. For all the unspoken words."

The weight of her promise settled over her, heavy but resolute. The understanding that had bloomed in the archive, nurtured by Beatrice's words, now rooted itself deeply within her. She was no longer just an inheritor of a cottage; she was the guardian of a memory, the keeper of a sacred trust.

# Chapter Six

The first frost of the season had hardened the ground, transforming the familiar earth into a brittle, unyielding surface. Elsie's boots, worn now and scuffed, crunched loudly over the frozen soil as she made her way from the cottage to the outdoor pump, then back towards the livestock pen, two heavy pails of water sloshing precariously in her gloved hands. Each step was a small, sharp protest against the cold. The chickens, usually bustling with irritable energy, were puffed up like feathered balls against the chill, their clucks muffled and peevish. In the far field, the sheep bleated in low, groaning tones, their breath pluming in the frigid air, a mournful chorus that seemed to echo the chill that had settled deep within Elsie's own bones.

She'd started rising earlier with the shortening days, long before the sun even dared to hint at warming the horizon. The work, relentless and demanding, helped. It was a brutal, necessary antidote to the insidious quiet that threatened to consume her. Chopping kindling, the axe biting into the wood with a satisfying thud. Turning the stubborn, frozen soil, each spadeful a small victory against the resistance of the earth. Mending the rickety gate hinges, her numb fingers struggling with the cold metal. Every task, every repetitive movement, served a crucial purpose: it kept her from drifting too far into the treacherous waters of her thoughts, from dwelling on Thomas and the terrifying, vast unknown that stretched between them. Her mind, left idle for even a moment, would conjure images of muddy trenches, distant explosions, the stark terror of a world at war. She no longer wrote in her journal during the day, no longer sought refuge in casual observations or weather notes. That quiet solace was now saved exclusively for the deep hours of night, for when the fire burned low to a gentle, pulsing glow, and the world outside felt thinner, more permeable, allowing the whispers of her heart to rise to the surface.

Margaret, the formidable farm manager, had grown gruffer with the deepening autumn. The strain of the war was wearing on her too, though she never articulated it, never spoke of the crushing weight of responsibility, the constant shortages, the relentless pressure to produce. Her lines were etched deeper, her shoulders a little more hunched, her movements a little wearier. A new girl had joined them just a fortnight ago—Gladys, barely sixteen, fresh from the unfamiliar bustle of Essex. She was a stark contrast to the farm's grim practicality, full of chatter and bright-eyed optimism that seemed almost offensive in its unwavering persistence. She whistled relentlessly while she worked, tuneless, cheerful melodies that grated on Elsie's raw nerves. She asked too many questions, her innocent curiosity a constant intrusion, and had already managed to lose three pairs of her government-issued gloves, a small but irritating act of carelessness.

Elsie didn't actively dislike Gladys. It was more a profound inability to connect, a chasm that had opened between her own inner turmoil and Gladys's unwavering cheerfulness. She found herself retreating more often, gravitating towards the farthest rows in the fields, or volunteering for the dirtier, more solitary jobs—mucking out the pigsty, cleaning the chicken coops. She simply couldn't hold light conversation anymore, couldn't engage in the idle chatter about rations or weather. Not when every fibre of her being, every beat of her heart, lived by the post, by the silent, agonizing expectation of a letter.

Each morning, before the first hint of dawn, she checked the small, scarred table near the cottage door, her breath held, willing a letter to be there, a white rectangle against the dark wood. And each morning, it remained bare, an empty space that mocked her hope. Seven weeks had passed, seven agonizing weeks, since Thomas's last message, since the crumpled, precious note that had confirmed his dangerous inland movement. The silence from him was a constant, gnawing presence, louder than any sound.

She listened for updates on the radio in the main house during meals, the crackle of static and the clipped, impersonal voice of the announcer becoming the soundtrack to her growing anxiety. Names of distant towns and obscure rivers. Enumerations of military units. The news was always delivered with a detached formality, a chilling objectivity that dehumanized the conflict. Casualties were simply numbers, grim statistics rattled off without inflection, not sons or brothers or lovers. And France? France, once a place of whispered promises and ancient cities, was now just a word, a theatre of operations, a terrifying abstraction that swallowed men whole.

A Fading Hope, A Renewed Promise
But then, one cold, grey afternoon, as she returned from feeding the goats in the distant pasture, her arms heavy from carrying the feed sacks, she saw it.

An envelope.

Slipped, almost carelessly, between two pieces of coal on the doorstep, as if left by some furtive, unseen hand. It was damp at the corners, softened by moisture, its edges slightly smudged. Her vision blurred for a moment, then sharpened with a terrible intensity. Her knees weakened beneath her, a sudden, alarming tremor running through her legs. She snatched it up, her fingers fumbling, and pressed it to her chest, as if the physical contact could somehow absorb the truth it contained, good or bad. It was his. It had to be. The shape, the weight, the indescribable feel of it in her hand.

She carried it inside, her steps slow and deliberate, a precious cargo. She didn't open it immediately. Not yet. She needed to prepare, to be ready. She waited until the fire was burning well, its flames leaping and dancing, casting warm, dancing shadows on the walls of her small cottage, pushing back against the encroaching cold and the deeper chill of her fear. The tea kettle hissed softly on the hob, a comforting, domestic sound. Only when the room felt adequately fortified, when the silence was deep and still, did she finally allow herself the indulgence.

The pages were creased, folded multiple times, and the ink was blotched in places, smudged as if by dampness or a hurried touch. But the writing was unmistakably his, the familiar slant, the strong, unwavering lines. Her eyes devoured the words, her heart thudding in her ears, a frantic drumbeat against the silence.

"Elsie," the letter began, simpler even than the last. He wasted no words.

"We're not where we were before. I can't say much, only that we've moved inland. Deeper. It's colder here now, a damp, penetrating cold, though I don't mind it much. My thoughts keep me warm enough. The trees here, the way they stand against the sky, they look exactly like the ones behind your cottage. The same gnarled branches, the same silent sentinels. That helps. It helps more than you know."

Elsie imagined him, wherever he was, looking at trees and seeing her orchard, seeing her. The image brought a fresh wave of tears to her eyes, though she blinked them back fiercely.

"I miss you. Not the kind of miss that fades or quiets with time or distance. Not the kind that a distraction can cure. The kind that builds, that grows heavier with each passing day. It's a constant ache, a dull throb beneath my ribs. There are nights I lie awake, staring up at the vast, indifferent sky, and I see your face more clearly than the stars above me. More clearly than the faces of the men beside me. Your eyes, Elsie. Your smile. They're burned into my mind."

The raw honesty of his confession, the depth of his longing, resonated with Elsie's own aching heart. He felt it too, this impossible, crushing distance.

"We don't know where we're going next. They don't tell us much, just move us, like pieces on a board. We are simply soldiers, waiting for orders, waiting for the next deployment. But I think of the orchard every morning, Elsie. As the sun rises, I close my eyes and I'm back there, beneath the twisted branches. I remember the way the light fell through the leaves, dappling your face. The sound of your laugh, that bright, sudden sound, when I stepped on that rotten apple and nearly fell flat on my face. You laughed. You really laughed."

A ghost of a smile touched Elsie's lips. She remembered that moment vividly, the clumsy fall, the unrestrained burst of mirth, a rare sound for her.

"You made me feel like the world could be gentle again, Elsie. Even in this, even now. You were a promise of something good, something quiet and true. Hold onto that thought for me. Hold onto the gentleness. Keep it safe."

And then, his name. "Thomas."

Elsie held the letter in her lap for a long time after she finished reading, the paper warm beneath her fingers, absorbing its words, its truth. She didn't cry. Not this time. The tears had been shed earlier, in anticipation, in fear. This was different. This was a fragile, precious connection across an impossible chasm. Instead, she folded it slowly, meticulously, tracing the familiar lines of his handwriting. She didn't put it back under the floorboard. This letter felt too urgent, too vital, to be hidden away immediately. Instead, she tucked it carefully behind the other, the one he had sent previously, the one she had decided to keep close, under the unassuming weight of the candle jar on the mantlepiece. A small, silent shrine to a love enduring against impossible odds.

That night, she lit a fresh candle, its small flame flickering bravely in the dim room, pushing back against the shadows. She took out her notebook, the familiar feel of the paper a comfort. She had to write. The words poured out, a torrent of desperate longing and fragile hope.

"My Dearest Thomas," she began, her pen scratching across the page, a new urgency in her own hand. "There was frost on the orchard this morning, a bitter lace upon the branches. I stood at the edge of it and thought of you—how you looked the first time you kissed me, beneath those very trees, like you were both wonderfully sure and terribly afraid, all at once. That moment is etched into my soul."

"We have a new girl now on the farm. Gladys. She talks enough for both of us, a relentless stream of chatter, innocent and bright. I find it harder and harder to speak, even when I want to. Even when I long to tell someone about you. It's as if too many words might make it all feel real, might make your absence concrete, insurmountable. Might make you feel farther away, a truth too painful to vocalize."

"I keep your handkerchief with me always. It is my constant companion. I've started sleeping with it under my pillow, clutching its soft, worn fabric in the dark. Sometimes I dream you're lying beside me, your breath warm on my neck, your arm around me, just like that last night in the cottage. Sometimes I wake abruptly, before the dreams can fully unfold, before the illusion breaks, and the emptiness of the bed is a cold shock."

"I haven't been sleeping well, the quiet of the night now too loud with my thoughts. Just tired in a different way now, a weariness that seeps into my very bones, beyond physical exertion. A weariness of the soul, perhaps."

"Come back to me, Thomas. Please. Just come back."

"Elsie"

She tied the letter with a fresh, crisp length of red ribbon, a symbol of her enduring love, and slipped it beneath the loose floorboard in her bedroom, a secret message awaiting its recipient, a prayer against the chaos.

As she knelt there, her hand resting on the smoothed wooden floorboard, something stirred in her lower belly—a faint, dull flutter. Not pain, exactly. Not discomfort. Just a strange pressure. A low, unfamiliar pull, like a subtle tightening, a faint whisper of movement deep within her. It was unlike anything she had felt before, a sensation that made her pause, her brow furrowed in a slight frown. She rested her hand over it, pressing lightly, trying to discern its nature, then shook her head, dismissing it. Likely just too many hours bent over fence posts, the constant strain of lifting heavy feed sacks, the ceaseless demands of the farm. Her body was tired, that was all.

Still, the sensation lingered, a faint, persistent awareness beneath the surface. It was a subtle, almost imperceptible shift in her own physical landscape, something new taking root. She banked the fire, carefully arranging the coals to keep them warm until morning, and climbed into bed, the words of her letter still echoing in her mind, Thomas's voice whispering in the darkness. Outside, the wind howled through the orchard, a mournful lament against the bare branches. And inside her, something else, profound and utterly new, had begun to take root.

# Chapter Seven

Sophie hadn't slept well. Again. The restless nights had
become a familiar companion since her arrival at the cottage,
each dawn finding her more weary than the last. She stirred
her tea absentmindedly in the chipped mug, its once warm
contents now entirely cold, a forgotten casualty of her
distracted thoughts. Her gaze was fixed on the rain tracing
slow, melancholic paths down the cottage windows, each
droplet leaving a shimmering trail before merging with
others. A fire crackled in the hearth behind her, its efforts
noble but ultimately futile against the persistent damp that
clung to the air, seeping into the old stone walls and
wrapping around her like a pervasive shroud. The letters lay
stacked neatly nearby on the kitchen table, bundled by week,
their contents a silent, compelling narrative. The latest one,
dated November 1941, Thomas's last heartbreaking message,
still sat beside her open journal, a poignant reminder of his
desperate longing.

She hadn't opened a new letter yet this morning. A strange,
insistent resistance held her back. It was as if the deeper she
delved into Elsie's story, the more inextricably tangled her
own life became with the past. As if each subsequent
revelation would make it harder to return to her own
fragmented existence, to the mundane demands of a life she
had deliberately fled. But wasn't that, she pondered, the very
point of being here? To shed the skin of her old self? To step
outside of everything familiar and comfortable, to embrace
the discomfort and the unknown, in order to figure out what
it truly meant to be Sophie again, unburdened by Daniel, by
London, by expectations? The answer, elusive and unsettling,
hovered just beyond her grasp.

Instead of reaching for another fragile envelope, she turned to her laptop, its glowing screen a jarringly modern presence in the rustic kitchen. She had begun the painstaking process of digitising Elsie's entries, both to preserve the fading ink from the ravages of time and to help her piece the convoluted story together, to create a timeline, a logical progression from the emotional chaos. Her fingers hovered over the keys, a momentary hesitation, then moved with slow, deliberate purpose, transcribing the words that had resonated so deeply within her.

"Nov 1941: He writes from inland. Says the trees remind him of hers. Says he misses her in a way that doesn't fade or quiet, but builds. A constant ache."

She paused, rereading the line, feeling the weight of Thomas's longing. Her thoughts, unbidden, moved from transcription to reflection, to the questions that had haunted her since first finding the hidden cache. She typed, the soft click of the keys a rhythmic counterpoint to the rain's steady drumming:

"This is not fiction. This was real. He was real. She was too. Their love wasn't some convenient plot device or doomed romantic fantasy crafted for a novel — this was the kind of fierce, unwavering love people spend their entire lives trying to recreate, trying to articulate. And yet they were quiet about it. Terribly, profoundly quiet. They told no one, or at least, the records hint at no one. Why? Why keep such a profound connection a secret? Why hide such a powerful truth?"

She sat back, leaning against the cold, unyielding wood of the chair. Maybe that was what haunted her most — the silence that surrounded their love, the deliberate act of concealment. It suggested a depth of circumstance, a complication that went beyond mere wartime separation.

A New Trail of Clues

The attic still held boxes she hadn't opened, forgotten relics of Elsie's life, gathering dust beneath the eaves. She'd been putting it off, telling herself that the mysteries unlocked from the floorboards and kitchen drawers had been enough for now, that the weight of discovery was already considerable. But now, after the recent revelations, after hearing Thomas's desperate longing echo in her mind, she felt something shift inside her, a new, undeniable pull. It was as if she owed it to them, to Elsie and Thomas, to look, to find every last piece of their story, to honour their hidden lives.

The steep, narrow attic stairs creaked mournfully under her feet with each ascending step, the old wood protesting softly under her weight. The air in the attic was colder than the main house, a stale, dust-laden chill that wrapped around her. Dust motes hung in the low light, dancing like tiny, ethereal spirits in the single, grimy window that pierced the gloom. She pulled the chain on the overhead bare bulb, and a sudden, harsh light flooded the cramped space, revealing a landscape of forgotten things. A few ancient trunks, their leather cracked and peeling like sun-baked skin. Two battered, canvas suitcases, their straps brittle. A stack of tea chests, their yellowed labels flaking, promising contents unknown. The air, heavy with the scent of old paper, mothballs, and a faint, sweet decay, pressed in on her.

She chose the smallest trunk first, its metal clasps stiff with disuse. With a grunt of effort, she wrestled it open. Inside were neatly folded old linens, yellowed with age, smelling faintly of lavender. A cracked picture frame, its glass clouded, lay face down. And beneath them, tucked away like a forgotten secret, a small bundle of receipts tied with rough garden twine, their paper brittle and fragile. She moved them aside, her fingers brushing against the rough surface of the trunk's bottom. And there it was: an envelope—thicker than Elsie's letters, weathered from time and perhaps damp, but crucially, unmarked. No sender, no recipient, no date. Just a plain, unassuming envelope.

Sophie sat cross-legged on the dusty floorboards, her heart hammering a frantic rhythm against her ribs. She opened it carefully, gingerly, as if the very act might shatter its contents.

Inside was a letter—addressed not from Elsie, as all the others had been, but to her.

It was from Thomas.

Her breath hitched. This was new. This was different. This was a letter Elsie had received, not one she had written for him.

"Elsie," the letter began, Thomas's bold, familiar script now infused with a new, raw intimacy, a voice reaching out from the distant past. "I'm writing this with the sound of rain against a tin roof and the ache of you still in my hands. The ache of every moment we shared, every touch, every whispered word."

Sophie imagined him, wherever he was, hunched over a scrap of paper, the rain drumming a relentless rhythm around him, his hands, the same hands that had held hers, aching with the memory of her.

"We marched through a field yesterday that smelled like late autumn — leaves decaying underfoot, the sharp tang of woodsmoke from a distant farm, and something else I couldn't quite place until I realised it was memory. It smelled like you, Elsie. Like the air around you in the orchard. A profound, aching scent of home."

He carried her scent. The thought brought a fresh sting to Sophie's eyes.

"There was a locket in my breast pocket. The silver one you gave me. I touched it so often, Elsie, just to feel you near, that the clasp has gone loose. Your picture inside is creased and worn, softened from how many times I've taken it out, just to look at your face, to remind myself of the quiet certainty you bring. A man in my company, a gruff sergeant, asked me who you were. I didn't hesitate. I told him you were my home. My true home, wherever I might be."

The declaration, so simple yet so powerful, resonated deep within Sophie. Elsie was his home. His sanctuary.

"We're heading east again. Deeper into it. They say we'll be mobile for weeks, maybe longer. The information is always vague, always shifting. I don't know if I'll get a chance to write again, not like this, not safely. But I wanted you to have this, Elsie. This final thought. In case I don't come back. In case the war claims me before I can return to you."

Sophie gasped, a small, choked sound. His words were a premonition, a terrible, heartbreaking prophecy.

"I'll try to write again soon, I promise. But I don't know when that will be. We're always on the move, always pushing forward, and the further we go, the harder it gets to find time, or paper, or safe places to send things from. The chaos is a constant companion now."

"But know this: I carry you with me in every step, in every breath, and I think of you more often than I can possibly say. You are my constant, Elsie. My calm in this relentless storm. My hope. My only peace."

And then, again, his stark, desperate signature: "Yours, Thomas."

Sophie sat completely still on the dusty attic floor, the letter clutched in her hands, her heart pounding a frantic, irregular rhythm. The silence of the attic, once merely cold and dusty, now felt profound, heavy with unspoken sorrow. The letter had been folded once, then again, and pressed between other forgotten things, perhaps slipped into a book or a small box. It was not hidden with the others under the floorboard. It had been set aside—protected, cherished, kept apart from the larger chronicle, perhaps because it was Elsie's last tangible piece of him, a final, sacred message from a man facing oblivion. Elsie must have tucked it away up here, a secret known only to her, away from the floorboard collection that served a different purpose.

She placed it gently in her lap, her fingers tracing the worn creases of the paper, as if through touch alone she could absorb its meaning, its weight.

Her gaze, still scanning the contents of the trunk, fell upon another bundle behind the first—not letters this time, but folded papers, tied not with ribbon or twine, but with a piece of faded, stiffened cloth.

One was a hospital record.

Her breath caught in her throat, a sharp, painful intake of air. The paper was thicker, official, stamped with the unmistakable insignia of a wartime hospital. Her eyes darted to the key words, the bold, terrifying truth.

"Mother: E. Hale"

The rest was blurred, obscured by what looked like old water damage, or perhaps simply the ravages of time. No child's name listed. No father's name. Just a date.

Spring 1942.

Sophie stood, her legs trembling, the world tilting slightly on its axis. Her heart was pounding, a deafening drumbeat in her ears. Elsie had had a child. In Spring 1942. Just months after Thomas had disappeared into the maw of war.

She placed the precious, horrifying paper gently beside Thomas's letter on the dusty floor and backed away slowly, as if too much sudden movement might disturb something sacred, might shatter the fragile truth she had just uncovered. She didn't want to jump to conclusions, didn't want to spin a story out of mere fragments. But part of her—the part that had always felt there was something missing in the clean, orderly narrative of the family she grew up in, the questions about Elsie that her father and mother had always sidestepped—began to stir, to hum with a terrifying, exhilarating recognition. The silence that had surrounded Elsie's life, the whispers, the vague hints from Marjorie and Beatrice, all coalesced into a single, undeniable conclusion.

Echoes of a Hidden Life

That evening, the cottage was bathed in the warm, flickering glow of the firelight. The rain had finally ceased, leaving a profound stillness outside. Sophie sat at the kitchen table, the laptop now closed, the letters and the newly discovered papers carefully laid out beside her open journal. The weight of the revelations pressed in on her, a physical sensation that made her feel both heavy and strangely, exhilaratingly, light.

"Today I found his words. Not hers this time, not the ones she poured out in private devotion, but his raw, desperate farewell. And they broke me. Not because they were sad, though they were. But because they were so utterly sure. So utterly devoted. He loved her, completely, unequivocally, even facing the impossible."

"She kept his voice safe here. She gave him a place to return to, a testament to their love, a promise etched in paper. And now, against all odds, all the years, all the silence, I have them both in my hands. His final message. Her secret truth."

She stopped writing, her pen poised above the page. She looked around the room, taking in the flickering shadows, the familiar comfort of the old cottage. It didn't feel empty anymore. It hadn't for days, not since she started reading the letters, not since Elsie's quiet spirit had begun to fill the spaces. But now, after the discovery of the hospital record, it felt more than merely inhabited—it felt alive. It felt inhabited by memory, by presence, by a profound, undeniable truth that had waited patiently, silently, long enough for someone to find it.

"There's more to this. I know it. There has to be. And I think, deep down, in the core of me that somehow recognises Elsie, I already know where it leads. I can feel the threads drawing together. But I'm not ready to say it yet. Not even to myself. Not out loud. The implications are too vast, too overwhelming."

She closed the book, its worn cover a familiar comfort, and added another log to the fire, watching the flames leap and consume the wood. The warmth spread through the room, a gentle counterpoint to the chill of the past.

In the profound quiet that settled over the cottage, she could almost hear his voice in the orchard, whispering across the decades, carrying the scent of autumn leaves and the ache of enduring love. She could almost feel Elsie's presence, her quiet strength, her fierce determination to protect the most precious secret of all. The cottage, once a refuge from her own broken life, had become a crucible of revelation, demanding that she confront not just Elsie's past, but her own unexamined present. The journey, she knew, had just truly begun.

# Chapter Eight

This chapter marks a crucial turning point for Sophie, shifting from passive discovery to active investigation, and introduces a new, potentially significant character. I will expand it to over 3000 words by intensifying Sophie's initial emotional state, her research process, the sensory details of the archive and Ben's character, and the subtle, nascent shift in Sophie's personal journey. The plot will remain exactly the same.

Chapter 8: The Search for Thomas

The following day, Sophie couldn't shake the weighty presence of what she'd found in the attic. The solitary letter from Thomas, a fragile cry from the heart of the war, and the stark, chilling revelation of the hospital record—"Mother: E. Hale"—had stirred something far deeper than mere intellectual curiosity. It was an urgent, almost primal need for understanding that hummed beneath the surface of her skin. The questions spun in her mind, relentless and insistent: Who was this child? Why was it unacknowledged? What tangled threads connected Thomas's disappearance to Elsie's hidden pregnancy? These thoughts lingered through her morning routine, shadowing her as she moved through the cottage, attempting to distract herself with the mundane. She tidied the small study, arranging books on shelves and wiping down dusty surfaces, and half-heartedly cleaned the kitchen, scrubbing the stubborn marks from the old wooden table. Yet, with every swipe of the cloth, every settled object, the unsolved mysteries of Elsie's past seemed to rise up, demanding her attention.

By mid-morning, with the persistent drizzle still blurring the world outside and the cottage holding a cool, damp chill,

Sophie found herself inevitably drawn back to her laptop in the kitchen. The radio murmured quietly in the background, a low, comforting hum of classical music, a stark contrast to the tumultuous thoughts raging within her. A cup of tea, made with fresh, hot water but now long forgotten, sat untouched beside her, a pale, still pool on the polished wood as she stared at the glowing screen. She had tried several vague search attempts, typing in combinations of "Thomas Ashford WWII missing," "Lincolnshire Land Army secrets," and "unregistered wartime births," only to be met with a frustrating deluge of too many misleading genealogy ads and irrelevant historical forums. It felt like shouting into a vast, digital void, the search engines offering only tangential connections.

Then, buried deep within a university's historical society page, a name, simple yet authoritative, struck a chord, resonating with a quiet sense of purpose:

Ben Taylor – Military History Researcher, Lincolnshire Historical Trust

The website was basic, stripped of any flashy graphics, but it exuded a quiet professionalism. He specialised, the modest blurb stated, in tracking wartime personnel and recovering lost records, particularly those relating to the less-documented aspects of military history. This was it. This was precisely what she needed. Sophie hovered her mouse over the generic contact form, her finger poised, then, on a sudden impulse, she clicked instead on his direct email address, a more personal, less formal route.

She kept the message short, concise, and to the point, stripping away any emotional preamble or speculative theories, presenting only the bare facts.

Hello,

I'm trying to trace a WWII soldier named Thomas Ashford, believed to have served and gone missing in France in 1942. I've recently discovered personal letters relating to him and am looking to understand what may have happened to him and if any official military records regarding his fate still remain.

Would you be available to speak at your earliest convenience to discuss this further? I am currently located in the Lincolnshire area.

Best,
Sophie Mercer

She hit send before she could overthink it, before the familiar doubts could creep in, before she could question the wisdom of contacting a complete stranger about such a deeply personal and potentially painful family secret. The email vanished, a digital whisper into the ether, leaving behind a sudden, quiet anticipation.

The Archivist
Ben replied that afternoon, his response arriving much faster than Sophie had anticipated, a ping that startled her from her contemplation of the rain-streaked orchard. His email was polite and professional, devoid of unnecessary formality, getting straight to the point. He expressed cautious interest in her discovery, acknowledging the rarity of finding such

personal documents. He offered to meet in person later in the week at the main Lincolnshire archives, where he worked part-time, suggesting it would be the most efficient way to access any relevant records. Sophie didn't hesitate. The very idea of an expert, someone who specialized in these very mysteries, was an immense relief. She quickly arranged to visit the following morning, the earliest available slot.

The archive building was tucked discreetly behind the bustling town hall, a solid, unassuming structure that had once served as the town's main library before being converted into a regional history centre. Its stone facade, though well-maintained, carried the subtle patina of age, a quiet dignity. Sophie arrived ten minutes early, her heart thrumming with a nervous energy she couldn't quite quell. Despite the compelling evidence she possessed, she was still not entirely sure what she was hoping to find. Closure? A missing piece? Or perhaps, just a deeper understanding of the secret that had shadowed Elsie's life?

Ben met her at the front desk, a large, polished oak counter that smelled faintly of lemon polish and old books. He was younger than she expected—early thirties, maybe mid-thirties—with messy dark blond hair that looked perpetually in need of a comb. He wore a navy jumper, its sleeves pushed carelessly to his elbows, revealing strong, capable forearms. A pair of wire-rimmed glasses perpetually slipped down his nose, requiring a frequent, absentminded push with his index finger every time he looked down at his notes or a document. His eyes, behind the lenses, were a warm, intelligent grey.

"Miss Mercer?" he asked, his voice low and pleasant, offering a quick, slightly crooked smile that put Sophie immediately at ease. It wasn't a professional, forced smile, but a genuine, slightly shy expression that softened his academic demeanour.

She stood, extending her hand. "Yes. Thank you so much for agreeing to meet me on such short notice." His handshake was firm, warm.

"Happy to help, Miss Mercer. This sounds like quite an intriguing case," he replied, his smile widening slightly. "Come on back—we've got a quiet room where we can go over what you've found in more detail. It's a bit less public than out here."

Sophie followed him, her boots making soft, almost reverent sounds on the polished linoleum floor. They passed through a labyrinth of towering, silent rows of archive boxes, shelves crammed with ancient bound ledgers, and wall-mounted maps, vast and intricate, depicting forgotten landscapes and altered boundaries. The air was cool and still, thick with the comforting, slightly musty scent of old paper and quiet history. Finally, they reached a side office, small but perfectly organized, its walls lined with more records and shelves of dusty catalogues. Ben pulled out a wooden chair for her at a large, uncluttered table, its surface worn smooth by countless hands and the passage of time.

"So, Thomas Ashford," he said, settling into the chair opposite her, pushing his glasses up his nose. He had a small, neat notebook open in front of him, a few penciled notes already visible. "That's not a name I've come across recently in my current research, but the records from 1941–42 are notoriously patchy in places, especially those pertaining to mobile units operating in the field. So many files were lost, so many men simply fell through the cracks of documentation. What do you know so far?" His tone was empathetic, professional, entirely non-judgmental.

Sophie hesitated, her hand instinctively reaching into her canvas bag. This was the moment. She pulled out the printed scan of Thomas's final, heartbreaking letter, folded neatly, and placed it on the table between them. She watched his face as he picked it up, unfolded it, and began to read.

Ben read it in silence, his expression shifting subtly as he absorbed the raw emotion etched into Thomas's words. His brow furrowed slightly in concentration, then softened, a fleeting shadow of empathy passing over his features. He pushed his glasses up his nose, paused, and reread a line, then the entire letter.

"That's... incredibly personal," he said quietly, his voice low, a note of genuine respect in his tone. He looked up at Sophie, his grey eyes thoughtful. "A rare find, indeed. Most personal correspondence like this didn't survive, let alone surface decades later."

"I found it in the attic of a cottage I inherited," Sophie explained, her voice gaining confidence, a newfound purpose. "The house belonged to my great-aunt, Elsie Hale. When I was clearing it out, I found dozens of letters she'd written—every single one addressed to Thomas Ashford, but never sent. This is the only letter I've found from him. His last one, I think."

Ben looked at her more closely now, his initial professional curiosity deepening into genuine intrigue. "That's quite a discovery, Miss Mercer. Quite extraordinary. I'm guessing these weren't officially archived or catalogued anywhere by your family?"

She shook her head, a slight smile touching her lips, a shared secret between her and Elsie. "No one knew they existed. Not even my father, Elsie's nephew. I think she kept them hidden all her life. Buried them, almost literally, under the floorboards."

He nodded slowly, his gaze thoughtful, a silent acknowledgment of Elsie's profound desire for privacy. "Well, this gives us a much stronger starting point than usual. I can run a more targeted search through the Home Guard rolls and any post-evacuation reports from units in that specific region of France during that timeframe. If he went missing in action, or was listed as captured or killed, there would likely be some record with the War Office archives, even if it's minimal. I've also got contacts within some of the larger military history societies who can help with specific battalion placements and movements around Caen in late 1941, early 1942. They might have access to more granular data than what's publicly available."

Sophie exhaled slowly, a long, quiet release of tension she hadn't realized she was holding. "That would be incredible, Ben. Truly. Thank you." The sheer possibility of finding answers, of finally understanding, was overwhelming.

Ben paused, his gaze softening, a hint of genuine curiosity in his grey eyes. "Do you mind if I ask why this matters so much to you, Miss Mercer? Beyond the family connection, of course. People find old letters all the time, but not many go to this much trouble."

Sophie hesitated, her hand brushing unconsciously against the cool, smooth edge of the table, a familiar gesture of contemplation. The question was fair, direct, and required an honest answer. She looked at the scan of Thomas's letter, then back at Ben, seeing the genuine interest in his face.

"Because I think their story matters," she began, her voice quiet but firm, finding a new clarity as she spoke. "And I think it was never told properly. Not in any official records, not in my family. There's something about the way she wrote to him—those desperate, hopeful, intensely personal letters. And now, the way he answered, his voice so clear in this last message. It's like they were the only two people left in the world, bound together by something unbreakable amidst all the chaos. And then something changed. His letters stopped. But she kept writing to him—quietly, faithfully, year after year, it seems. Like she was still waiting for him. Still believing."

Ben leaned back slightly in his chair, his head tilted, watching her with a thoughtful intensity. He wasn't just listening to her words; he seemed to be listening to the emotion behind them. "You're not just trying to find out what happened to him, are you?" he observed, his voice gentle.

"No," she admitted, meeting his gaze directly. The raw honesty felt strangely liberating. "I'm trying to understand why it was kept quiet. Why she never told anyone, not even her own family. What else she didn't say. What else she had to hide." The last thought, the unspoken child, hovered between them, a truth she wasn't ready to vocalize just yet.

He nodded slowly, a deep, contemplative expression on his face. He picked up the scan of Thomas's letter again, his thumb gently tracing the faded ink of Thomas's name. "It's a powerful narrative, isn't it? The untold stories are often the most profound." He looked up at her, his expression resolute. "I'll help you dig, Miss Mercer. And I'll treat it with the care and discretion it deserves. This isn't just research; it's a restoration."

Sophie smiled, a genuine, unburdened smile that spread across her face, surprising her with its ease. A wave of immense relief washed over her, a loosening of the tight knot in her chest. For the first time in what felt like forever, she wasn't alone in this quest.

As they stood to leave the small office, Ben glanced at her, a hint of something more casual in his gaze. "Would you like to grab a coffee, Miss Mercer? There's a place across the square that does terrible cappuccinos, I'm afraid, but they make a truly magnificent flapjack. And it's still raining." He gestured towards the window with a wry smile.

Sophie blinked, then a soft, unbidden laugh escaped her lips. The offer was unexpected, a sudden ray of warmth cutting through the academic intensity of their meeting. "Sure," she said, the word coming easily. "Why not. A terrible cappuccino and a great flapjack sounds exactly like what I need."

They stepped out of the archive building and into the crisp afternoon light, the air still damp with the lingering rain, the wind carrying the promise of more. As they walked together toward the café, a new, lighter sensation stirred within Sophie. Not heavy with grief. Not complicated with past regrets. Just the flicker of something unexpected. Something akin to a quiet, unfamiliar curiosity, not just about Elsie's past, but about her own unforeseen present.

# Chapter Nine

This chapter is incredibly poignant, focusing on Elsie's internal struggle and the subtle, yet profound, dawning of a new reality. I will expand it to over 3000 words by intensifying her physical and emotional sensations, detailing her daily routine and avoidance tactics, elaborating on her perception of Gladys and Margaret, and heightening the drama and finality of Thomas's last letter. The plot points will remain unchanged.

Lincolnshire, December 1941

Elsie woke before dawn with the metallic, unsettling taste of copper in her mouth. It was a bitter, pervasive flavour that clung to her tongue, intensifying the churning in her stomach. This was the third morning in a row she'd woken with the same queasy dread, her stomach tight and sour, a dull, persistent ache that refused to dissipate. The darkness in the small, unheated bedroom pressed in on her, amplifying the clammy discomfort. She sat on the edge of her narrow bed, the cold air biting at her exposed skin, pressing her hands firmly into her thighs, digging her nails into the rough wool of her nightdress, breathing slowly and deliberately through her nose until the wave of nausea, like a cold tide, finally receded, leaving her weak and trembling.

It had to be the cold, she told herself, trying to reason away the unsettling sensations. The relentless, seeping damp that clung to everything in the cottage, the biting wind that whistled through the ill-fitting windowpanes. Or the ever-present stress of the war, the constant, low thrum of anxiety that vibrated through every waking moment. Or perhaps, she rationalized, it was simply the heavy, indigestible biscuits she'd unwisely eaten before bed, too close to midnight, an attempt to fill the gnawing emptiness that often accompanied her restless nights. She clung to these mundane explanations, pushing away the nascent, more frightening possibilities that flickered at the edges of her consciousness.

She dressed slowly, each movement an effort, pulling her thickest wool jumper over her blouse, its familiar rough texture a small comfort against her skin. She wrapped a scratchy wool scarf tightly around her neck, tucking it snugly to ward off the insidious cold before stepping outside into the pre-dawn gloom. The air was sharp, biting, stealing her breath in small, frosty clouds. The ground was frozen solid, unforgiving underfoot, each step a jarring impact that sent a dull ache up her shins. She fetched water from the pump, the metal handle stiff and groaning in protest as she wrenched it downwards, the icy water a shocking baptism for her numb hands.

Work helped. It always did. The relentless physical demands of the farm provided a much-needed, brutal distraction. She moved with a practiced efficiency now, her muscles toned and hardened from months of labour. She fed the clucking hens, scattering grit with a practiced flick of her wrist, their agitated movements a welcome, mindless rhythm. She checked the fence line for gaps, her eyes scanning for weaknesses, her mind focused entirely on the immediate task. She'd quietly, almost instinctively, taken to doing more than her assigned share, volunteering for the heaviest, dirtiest, or most remote tasks, keeping her body in constant motion. Margaret, typically observant, never acknowledged it, her focus entirely consumed by the farm's ceaseless demands. Perhaps she simply considered it Elsie's nature.

Gladys, the new girl from Essex, hummed cheerfully nearby as she stacked kindling, her bright optimism utterly unaffected by the biting cold or the grim realities of the war. Her tuneless melodies, a childlike, persistent drone, seemed to float through the crisp air, a stark counterpoint to Elsie's internal turmoil. Elsie caught sight of her from the corner of the barn, Gladys's youthful face aglow with an almost unsettling, unburdened happiness, and quickly, almost instinctively, turned away, retreating deeper into the shadows of the barn.

Back in the cottage, the air, though warmer than outside, still held a pervasive dampness. Elsie removed her worn gloves, her fingers stiff and chilled, and sat down at the small kitchen table. Her journal was waiting for her, its blank pages a silent invitation, a space for the thoughts she could articulate nowhere else. So too was the growing stack of letters she'd already written and hidden beneath the floorboard, a silent testament to her enduring hope and gnawing fear. No new post had come for weeks, not since Thomas's brief, precious message confirming his inland movement. The silence from him stretched between them like a thread pulled too tight, thin and taut, threatening to snap at any moment. It was a silence that spoke volumes, a chilling absence that was louder than any battle cry.

She uncapped her pen, its familiar weight comforting in her hand, and began to write, the words forming slowly at first, then gaining a quiet momentum.

"My Dearest Thomas," she began, her pen scratching faintly on the paper. "I dreamt of you last night. So vividly. You were walking through the orchard again, our orchard, your coat buttoned all wrong, just like that first time, and your boots tracking mud all over the cottage floor. I didn't mind. I didn't care about the mud, about the mess. I just knelt and kissed your muddy face, holding you close, feeling the warmth of you, the reality of you. It felt so real, Thomas. So terribly real."

"It's quieter here now, in some ways. A new girl, Gladys, joined us from Essex. She sings while she works—badly, I must confess, but I suppose it helps her, helps her keep the fears at bay. I try to stay away from her chatter, retreat into myself. I think she knows something's wrong, something is different with me, but doesn't know what. I'm not even sure I do, Thomas. Not entirely. Not yet."

"I've been so tired lately. More than usual. A profound, bone-deep exhaustion that sleep doesn't seem to touch. I thought it was just the early frost, biting at my bones, or the endless, long nights that stretch into empty hours. But it's a deeper kind of tired, Thomas. A quiet hum under the surface of my skin, a constant, low awareness. My hands, usually so steady with the farm work, shake some mornings, a fine tremor that I can't control. I've stopped mentioning it to anyone, lest they ask too many questions. I wear long sleeves. I tell myself it's the cold. But I know, deep down, it's not just the cold."

"Please write soon. Even just a line, Thomas. A single word. Anything. This silence, it's becoming unbearable."

"Elsie"

She folded the letter with meticulous care, her fingers tracing the neat lines of her own script. She walked upstairs, her steps heavy, to tuck it under the same loose floorboard in her bedroom, where the growing collection of her unspoken hopes and fears lay hidden. The floorboards creaked louder lately, a mournful groan under her weight, as if they too felt the strain of her secret. She pressed them back gently into place, then rested her hand there a moment longer than necessary, a silent, desperate prayer for Thomas's safety, for his return.

## An Unspoken Concern

Later that week, as the days continued to shrink and the cold deepened its grip on the land, Gladys, surprisingly astute despite her youthful exuberance, cornered Elsie in the dim, hay-scented interior of the barn. The air was thick with the dust of dried straw and the faint, sweet smell of silage.

"You alright, Elsie?" Gladys asked, her bright, innocent eyes fixed on Elsie's face, brushing stray pieces of hay from her uniform sleeves. Her voice was gentle, lacking its usual boisterous cheer.

"I'm fine," Elsie replied too quickly, her voice sharper than she intended, a reflexive shield snapping into place. She turned away, pretending to adjust a harness on the wall.

Gladys didn't move. "You've gone quiet. Quieter than usual, I mean. Even for you. Margaret's been watching you, you know. She's worried. She asked if you were eating properly."

"I'm just tired," Elsie insisted, the familiar excuse feeling flimsy even to her own ears. The deeper kind of tiredness, the one she now carried like a secret weight, was impossible to explain.

Gladys frowned, her brow furrowed with a genuine concern that surprised Elsie. "You look pale, Elsie. And you've lost a bit of colour in your cheeks. Not meanin' it nasty, mind. Just... if you need help, I can cover for you a bit. With the feeding and such. I don't mind. You've been doing extra for weeks now." Her offer was sincere, a moment of unexpected, unsolicited kindness.

Elsie blinked, caught off guard. It was the first kindness, the first genuine, empathetic gesture she'd received in days, perhaps weeks, since Thomas's last letter had left her feeling adrift. A warmth, faint but distinct, bloomed in her chest, a counterpoint to the persistent nausea. "I'll manage, Gladys," she said, her voice softer this time, a note of gratitude in its tone.

Gladys nodded, though her gaze remained fixed on Elsie. "Suit yourself, then." But she lingered, brushing more imaginary hay from her sleeves, watching Elsie with a quiet, observant intensity as Elsie turned away. Elsie could feel her gaze on her back, a tangible presence, and for a moment, the solitude she had so carefully cultivated felt less like protection and more like a fragile, isolating barrier.

### The Unmistakable Truth

By Friday, the nausea was worse, a constant, churning misery that made the thought of food unbearable. She skipped breakfast entirely, the very smell of cooking lard and fried bread making her stomach revolt. Instead, she walked the orchard, seeking the cold, clean air, the familiar comfort of the gnarled trees. The frost crackled beneath her boots with every step, a sharp, crystalline sound. The sky was a uniform, oppressive grey, heavy with unshed rain or perhaps snow.

She walked slowly, her steps faltering slightly, her hands pressed instinctively to her lower belly. She leaned against the gnarled, rough trunk of the central tree—their tree, the one where they had shared apples and whispered hopes, where he had kissed her—and closed her eyes, breathing deeply, trying to steady the frantic beating of her heart.

She hadn't let herself name it yet. The possibility. The terrifying, exhilarating truth that had been forming in the quiet corners of her mind, like condensation on a cold pane of glass, slowly, inexorably, becoming clearer. The signs were there, undeniable and insistent. The persistent nausea. The overwhelming, bone-deep tiredness that no amount of rest could assuage. The subtle, unfamiliar pressure in her lower belly, the low, unfamiliar pull she had dismissed as strain from work. Her body, usually so predictable in its rhythms, had begun to betray a new, profound secret.

She wasn't just tired. She wasn't just cold. Something had irrevocably changed. A new life, small and vulnerable, was stirring within her, a tiny, defiant spark in the midst of a world at war. The realization, quiet and profound, settled over her like a heavy cloak. Fear, raw and potent, mingled with a faint, incredulous wonder.

When she returned to the cottage, her mind reeling, her body aching, a letter was waiting on the kitchen table. It lay there, a lone, stark white against the dark wood. Margaret must have left it there, a silent messenger.

She tore it open with trembling hands, her heart leaping with a desperate, familiar hope. It was thin, just a single sheet.

It would be the last letter she ever received from him. A terrible, premonitory dread settled over her, a cold certainty that this was the final thread, the last whisper.

"Elsie," it began, his script a little rougher, hurried.

"We're moving again. Hard to say where, but it feels farther from home than ever. Further from the orchard, further from you. I think of you often, every waking moment, every desperate hour—how your hands feel in mine, the warmth of your skin, the way you tilt your head when you're thinking, that thoughtful frown that creases your brow."

"The nights are long and loud now, filled with the constant drone of planes, the distant rumble of shelling. I wear your locket under my shirt, against my skin, and touch it when I need stillness, when the world around me threatens to overwhelm. It is my only anchor, Elsie."

"I don't know when I'll write again. Maybe soon, if fate is kind. Maybe not for a while. The chaos is constant. The silence might be long. But know this, Elsie: I'm still here. Still fighting. Still thinking of the orchard, of our tree, of the sunlight dappling the ground beneath it. Of you. Always of you."

"Yours, Thomas"

Elsie sat down, the letter clutched tightly in her lap, the paper a brittle testament to his enduring presence. She closed her eyes and let his words wash over her, a wave of profound sorrow and desperate, fierce love. He was still out there. Still holding on. Still fighting. Still thinking of her, of their shared moments, of the quiet sanctuary they had found.

She rose, moving with a new, deliberate slowness, as if sensing the precious cargo she now carried. She lit a single candle on the mantle, its flame flickering bravely against the encroaching dusk. And then, with a profound sense of purpose, she picked up her pen, dipped it in the ink, and began to write. To the father of the child she now knew nestled within her. To the man who was still out there, holding onto the memory of her, of their quiet orchard. To the love that refused to be silenced, no matter the distance, no matter the war.

# Chapter Ten

The phone rang just after seven, its shrill, insistent summons slicing through the quiet morning. Sophie stood in the kitchen of the cottage, halfway through tidying up breakfast, the faint aroma of toast and instant coffee lingering in the air. The radio hummed low in the background, a gentle murmur of classical music providing a soothing backdrop to the grey, drizzly dawn outside. When the call came, a number she didn't recognize on the small, reconnected landline, she nearly didn't answer. No one ever called the landline. It had only been reconnected last week, a concession to the slow, sometimes unreliable internet in this remote corner of Lincolnshire.

She picked it up, a cautious "Hello?" escaping her lips.

"Sophie?" Her mother's voice, usually steady and composed, cracked, thin and tight with something unspoken, something profoundly wrong. The single word, her name, conveyed an immediate, chilling dread.

"Mum? What's wrong?" Sophie's heart lurched, a cold knot forming in her stomach.

"It's Dad," her mother said, the words tumbling out, rushed and desperate. "He collapsed at the house. Just... just fell. The ambulance took him in. They think... they think it was a heart attack. A massive one."

Sophie went utterly, terrifyingly still. The world seemed to shrink to the size of the telephone receiver pressed against her ear. The humming radio, the scent of coffee, the drizzle outside—all of it faded, replaced by a deafening roar in her ears, a static of rising panic. Her father. Indestructible. Solid. Her mind refused to process the words, searching for a flaw in the sentence, a way to render it false.

"Which hospital?" she managed to croak, her voice a thin, reedy sound she barely recognized as her own.

"St. Mary's. They... they worked on him in the ambulance. They're still working."

"I'll leave now." The words were automatic, a primal response to a primal fear.

The drive blurred into a terrifying, monochrome sequence. The familiar winding country roads, usually a source of quiet contemplation, became a tunnel, a frantic race against an unseen clock. Her fingers clenched the steering wheel, knuckles white, the plastic hard and cold beneath her grip. Sleet began to patter against the windscreen, a soft, insidious drumming that mirrored the frantic beat of her own heart. The wipers scraped rhythmically, clearing small arcs of visibility, but her vision was narrowed, focused only on the endless grey ribbon of asphalt ahead. She didn't turn on the radio, couldn't bear any external noise. She didn't let her thoughts form words, pushed back against the encroaching tide of fear and what-ifs. Just kept driving, pushing the old car faster than she should, driven by a desperate, silent mantra: Please, please, please be okay. Please don't be gone. Please.

She arrived at the hospital ninety minutes later, the sleet having turned the concrete outside the emergency entrance into a treacherous, icy surface. Her boots slipped, jarring her, but she barely noticed. The fluorescent lights inside, harsh and unforgiving, stung her eyes as she stepped over the threshold, her chest burning from the cold and the raw, suffocating panic that had become her only companion. The air smelled of antiseptic and stale coffee, a sterile, uncaring environment that felt alien and hostile.

The receptionist, her face impassive behind the counter, barely looked up when Sophie gave her name. Her voice was flat as she pointed down a long, white corridor. Her mother was waiting there, a small, hunched figure seated on a hard plastic chair.

"Sophie," her mum said softly, her voice strained, a raw whisper of unshed tears. She rose, her movements slow, heavy, as if carrying an invisible weight.

The expression on her mother's face told Sophie everything. It was a look of profound, unbearable grief, a mask of uncomprehending shock that mirrored her own deepest fears. The eyes, red-rimmed and swollen, held a terrible, final knowledge.

"No," Sophie whispered, the single syllable ripped from her throat, a choked, desperate sound. The world seemed to tilt, the fluorescent lights momentarily swimming above her.

"I'm sorry, darling," her mum said, her hand reaching out, cold and trembling, to grasp Sophie's arm. "He was gone before they could stabilise him. Just... went. Quickly. They said he wouldn't have felt much."

It didn't register at first. The words hung in the air, abstract and meaningless. Sophie looked past her mother, her gaze frantically searching the corridor, expecting someone to step out from a room, a doctor, a nurse, and say it was a mistake. That he was resting. That they'd made a wrong call. That he was strong, indestructible.

But no one came. Only the quiet hum of the hospital, the distant clatter of trolleys, the soft murmurs of other people's lives. Her mum's hand tightened on her arm, a gentle, guiding pressure, and she led Sophie slowly, inexorably, towards a quiet room, a door already ajar.

The Unbearable Stillness
He lay on the bed, pale, still, impossibly quiet. The crisp white sheet was pulled up to his chest, his hands resting on top, his face turned slightly towards the door. The machines were already off, disconnected, silent. The tangle of cables and wires removed. Just a man, motionless and unnaturally peaceful, and the raw, throbbing memory of his life, his movement, his vibrant presence.

Sophie stood at his bedside, numb, a profound, chilling emptiness spreading through her. Her father. He had always seemed so utterly indestructible to her. Strong, stoic, complicated in his quiet way—but fundamentally, immovably solid. A fixed point in her chaotic world. Now he looked like someone else entirely. Smaller. Fragile. Finished. The very idea of him being "finished" was inconceivable.

Her mother stood beside her, just as still, her arms folded tight across her chest, her gaze fixed on the man on the bed. She didn't speak, didn't attempt to offer comfort or explanation, perhaps because there was none. Only the shared, suffocating weight of their loss.

Sophie wanted to cry, wanted the floodgates to open, for the tears to wash away the crushing numbness, but nothing came. Her eyes remained dry, her throat tight and aching. Just the hollow, thudding echo of regret, a relentless drumbeat in her mind. Regret for words unsaid, for questions unasked, for the distance she had kept. She thought of Elsie's letters, of Thomas's desperate last words, of the profound, fragile nature of unspoken love.

She reached for his hand, hesitated, then clasped it. It was cold, so utterly, irrevocably cold, the warmth of life long gone. "I should've come back sooner," she said under her breath, the words a raw, desperate whisper of self-recrimination.

Her mum squeezed her shoulder, a gentle, comforting pressure. "He knew you loved him, darling. He always did."

But Sophie wasn't sure if she believed it. Not really. Not truly. Not in the face of this stark finality, this abrupt, unyielding silence.

She stared at the man who had raised her. The man who had teased her endlessly about her messy handwriting, yet taught her, patiently, meticulously, how to change a tyre, how to check the oil, how to understand the inner workings of an engine. The man who stayed up with her the night before her driving test, pacing the hallway, murmuring encouragement while she desperately memorized road signs. The man who, when she was sick as a child, made exactly three different kinds of toast—burnt, lightly toasted, and barely warm—because he couldn't remember which one had helped last time, and wanted to cover all possibilities. The man whose quiet presence had been a constant, unwavering anchor in her life.

Now he was simply part of the past. Gone, like a beloved photograph left out in the relentless rain—still recognizable, the faint outlines of his being there, but blurred at the edges, slowly fading, becoming indistinct, no longer sharp and vibrant.

They left the room quietly, the silence between them thick with grief. The nurses at the station nodded with polite, practiced sympathy, their faces kind but distant. Sophie didn't remember the walk back to the car, the automatic movements of putting one foot in front of the other. It was a blank.

The rain had stopped, but the sky felt heavy, a bruised, oppressive grey that pressed down on the world. Back in the passenger seat beside her mum, the engine murmuring softly, Sophie said nothing. Her mother didn't either. They just sat together, both staring ahead through the windscreen, the vast, unbearable weight of loss filling every inch of the space between them, a silent, shared burden.

The Ritual of Grief
The funeral was scheduled for the following Tuesday, a swift, almost brutal efficiency demanded by the circumstances. Sophie stayed at her mother's house in the meantime, the familiar, comforting walls now imbued with a profound sadness. The days passed in a series of disorienting fragments—the incessant ringing of the phone, punctuated by hushed conversations with distant relatives, their voices choked with sympathy. Silent, tasteless meals, eaten from plates that seemed too heavy, too real. Piles of paperwork,

official documents and condolences, that she didn't have the energy or the will to read, their words blurring into meaningless lines. Her childhood bedroom, where she retreated nightly, hadn't changed in years. Posters on the wall, faded rock bands staring out with youthful defiance. A bookshelf crammed full of dog-eared paperbacks, the spines cracked and worn from countless rereads. It felt like stepping into a room abandoned in a hurry, suspended in time, filled with the ghosts of her younger self.

On the fourth night, after another day of murmured condolences and forced pleasantries, she lay awake in the dark, listening to the old boiler tick and groan down the hall, its mechanical sighs a lonely sound in the quiet house. Her mother had gone to bed hours earlier, utterly exhausted from the long line of mourners who had filtered through the house all day, each one offering well-meaning but ultimately inadequate words of comfort.

Sophie stared at the ceiling, seeing not the familiar plaster, but the stark, unyielding truth of loss. Grief was strange. It didn't hit all at once, not like a sudden, cataclysmic storm. It came in waves—some strong enough to knock her off her feet, leaving her gasping for breath, others just a quiet ache under the ribs, a dull, persistent throb. It was a tide, ebbing and flowing, sometimes receding enough to allow for moments of numb normality, sometimes crashing over her with overwhelming force.

She wondered, with a fresh surge of sorrow, if her father had truly known how much she still needed him. How much she relied on his quiet strength, his unwavering presence, even from a distance. She wondered if anyone ever did, truly, fully, understand the depth of their impact until they were gone.

The thought echoed the unspoken longing she had found in Elsie's letters, the profound connection that only death could truly illuminate.

The morning of the funeral was bright and cold, a cruel contrast to the internal gloom. Frost coated the lawn outside the church, sparkling like a million tiny diamonds in the sharp sunlight. Inside, the pews filled slowly, a sombre procession of friends, neighbours, and colleagues, their faces etched with sympathy. Sophie sat in the front row with her mother, their shoulders almost touching, her hands clenched tightly in her lap, her body rigid with a desperate control.

She didn't cry during the service, not when the eulogies were read, not when the hymns were sung in mournful tones. She didn't cry at the graveside, not as the coffin was lowered into the frozen earth, not when the first handfuls of soil rained down with a dull thud. Her eyes remained dry, her face a mask of carefully constructed composure. But when they returned to the house, after the final goodbyes at the graveside, and she stepped into the quiet kitchen, the familiar heart of their home, and saw his old, worn coat still hanging on the back of the door, just as he'd left it—that was when she broke.

The sight of it, mundane and utterly normal, a silent testament to a life that had simply stopped, unleashed the dam. She sank into a chair, not caring where, and buried her face in her hands, ragged, choking sobs finally tearing from her throat, wrenching her body with their force. The grief, raw and primal, consumed her. Her mother found her there ten minutes later, a silent, comforting presence. She didn't say a word, didn't try to offer platitudes. Just sat beside her, quiet and close, her own hand reaching out to rest gently on Sophie's shaking shoulder, sharing the unbearable burden.

That evening, the house still held the faint echoes of mourners, the lingering scent of lilies and sorrow. Sophie, her eyes swollen and aching, quietly packed her bag. The cottage called to her, a silent promise of solitude, of a space where she could begin to understand, to heal.

"I think I need to go back to the cottage," she told her mother, her voice still rough with unshed tears. "Just for a few days. I... I need to be there."

Her mum didn't argue. Her eyes, though still clouded with grief, held a deep understanding. "I understand, darling. Go. Do what you need to do."

Sophie hugged her tightly at the door, a desperate, clinging embrace. Neither of them said what they were really thinking: that the cottage now felt like a refuge from the crushing weight of their immediate loss, a place where Elsie's story might offer a different kind of solace.

She drove back to the village in silence, the road stretching ahead, empty and grey under the gathering dusk. The car, once a frantic escape vehicle, now felt like a slow, deliberate journey into the quiet heart of her own pain. Her thoughts were anything but empty, a swirling vortex of memories, of questions, of Elsie, of Thomas, of her father.

When she reached the cottage and stepped inside, the familiar coolness of the air wrapped around her. The warmth from the hearth, which she had carefully banked before leaving, had long faded, leaving only a lingering ghost of warmth. She dropped her bag by the door with a soft thud and crossed to the fireplace, its grate now cold and dark.

She sat for a long time on the rug, staring into the empty grate, arms folded tightly around herself, rocking slightly, a small, lost figure in the vast, silent room. The weight of her father's death, the lingering questions about Elsie's life, pressed down on her.

Then she whispered to the empty room, her voice raw and breaking, "I'm sorry."

She didn't know if she meant it for her dad, for the unspoken words, the missed opportunities. Or for Elsie, for the profound sadness of her hidden life and her unanswered love. Or for the terrifying, bewildering things she had yet to understand about her own family, about the secrets that had been kept.

Maybe all three. And perhaps, for herself, for the fragile, broken person she felt herself to be.

# Chapter Eleven

The morning after her return to the cottage was still and pale, painted in muted shades of grey that seeped through the windows. Sophie woke late for once, a rare luxury, having drifted into a dreamless, heavy sleep that had offered oblivion rather than true rest. For a few moments, she lay utterly still in bed, staring up at the rough-hewn wooden beams above her, letting the profound quiet settle over her. No sharp, intrusive hospital noises, no sympathetic murmurs from well-meaning visitors, no incessant ring of her mother's phone. Just the profound, encompassing silence of the cottage, save for the soft, whispering rustle of wind through the bare branches of the trees outside, a gentle, almost meditative sound.

She didn't feel rested, not in the sense of being refreshed or invigorated. She felt, rather, paused. Like someone had pressed her life's brake pedal with an unseen foot and hadn't yet released it. The frantic, desperate energy of the last few days had simply ceased, leaving her suspended in an unsettling limbo. Grief hadn't hit her in crashing, overwhelming waves, not yet, not in the way she had read about or seen in films. Instead, it just sat in her chest, a smooth, impossibly heavy stone she couldn't shift, a dull, constant pressure that anchored her to the moment, preventing any forward motion. It was a suffocating weight that made every breath feel shallow.

After dressing in warm, comfortable clothes and making a strong cup of tea, its steam briefly fogging the cool kitchen air, she found herself standing in the doorway between the kitchen and the sitting room, a silent sentinel, simply looking around. The fireplace was cold, its grate black and empty, mirroring the chill that permeated the cottage. The scent of dust and dry stone, a faint, ancient smell, still clung to the air, a reminder of the house's long history. It was strange, she mused, how quickly this place, once so alien and neglected, had become familiar. Familiar and, more surprisingly, safe, in a way her mother's grief-stricken house hadn't felt. Here, there were no photos of her father smiling from mantles, no jackets slung carelessly over chairs, no stacks of unopened condolence cards bearing the weight of unspoken sympathy. Just space. A vast, quiet expanse where she could simply exist, unobserved and unburdened by the immediate demands of mourning.

She didn't open any new letters. Not yet. The very idea of Thomas's confident handwriting, of Elsie's aching, raw words, felt too sharp, too potent in the immediate wake of her father's death. It felt disrespectful somehow, to dive into someone else's historical grief when her own was still so excruciatingly fresh, so raw. The thought of confronting such profound love and loss, however distant, was simply too much. But that didn't mean she could simply sit still. The stillness of the cottage, though a balm, also threatened to become a suffocating prison for her own spiralling thoughts.

Instead, she pulled out an old, soft cloth she'd found in a drawer and began to dust. Not with any particular intention of achieving true cleanliness, but as something to do with her hands. She ran the cloth along the windowsills, the rough grain of the wood familiar beneath her fingers, wiping away the accumulated film of grey dust. She worked her way along the skirting boards, feeling the subtle unevenness of the old timber, then meticulously cleaned the corners where tenacious cobwebs had slowly, patiently reclaimed their space, spinning intricate, ghostly webs in the quiet neglect. It wasn't about cleaning, not really. It was about controlling something. Anything. It was a focused, repetitive motion that demanded just enough attention to keep her mind from splintering, to anchor her to the present, to the tangible act of brushing away the accumulated layers of time.

Mid-morning gave way to noon without her even realising, the sun, if it was there at all, lost behind the persistent, unyielding clouds. The kettle boiled again on the hob, its whistle a sudden, piercing sound in the quiet kitchen, pulling her back to the present. She poured herself another cup of tea, but forgot it, steaming and fragrant, on the counter, its warmth diffusing into the cold air. She moved through the cottage, a restless ghost in the house of a ghost. In the sitting room, she ran her fingers along the spines of old, dusty books, their titles indistinct, and opened drawers she had already emptied twice before, searching for nothing in particular, yet driven by a subconscious need to uncover. She checked behind the heavy, faded curtains, inside empty jars on the mantelpiece, even underneath the worn, patterned rug in the centre of the room, her actions a quiet, almost ritualistic search for an unknown something.

Her mind, despite her efforts at distraction, drifted often. To the stark, cold brevity of the funeral. To her mother's tight, unyielding silence, a grief too deep for words. To her father's empty coat, still hanging on the back of the kitchen door at her mother's house, a heartbreakingly mundane testament to his sudden absence. The way his shoes had looked, still lined up neatly under the stairs, as if he might come back any second to put them on, to walk back into their lives. The mundane details of loss were often the most brutal.

At one point, she found herself standing in the middle of the room, a large, heavy photo album in her hands, its cracked leather binding cool and smooth beneath her fingers. She had no memory of how she'd gotten it down from the shelf, how it had come into her possession. She didn't open it. The thought of confronting another visual archive of a past, perhaps her own, felt too overwhelming. Just stared at the cracked leather binding, running her thumb across the surface, a silent communion with the unviewed memories within.

A New Concealment
It wasn't until she moved a stack of faded, yellowed magazines beside the hearth, intending to stack them more neatly, that she noticed something unusual. The baseboard behind the old cabinet, which she had previously overlooked in her cursory tidying, didn't sit quite flush against the wall. It was a subtle imperfection, barely discernible, but her restless gaze, now hyper-aware of every hidden crevice, every secret space, caught it. A faint, almost imperceptible gap. She pulled the heavy, dust-coated unit gently aside, scraping it slightly across the floorboards, exposing the join.

A slim wooden panel, slightly warped with age, ran along the lower part of the wall, distinct from the regular skirting board. One edge had a faint, almost invisible groove, as if designed for a fingernail, or a thin blade. It was too precise, too deliberate, to be a mere flaw in construction. Another hidden space. Elsie's secrets seemed to be layered within these very walls, waiting patiently to be found.

Sophie knelt down, her knees protesting slightly on the cold floorboards, her heart beginning to thump with a slow, heavy rhythm against her ribs. This was it. Another piece.

She slid her fingernail carefully under the groove and tugged. The panel gave way with a reluctant, drawn-out creak, a soft sigh of protest from the old wood, revealing a narrow, dark cavity within the wall itself. The air that emerged from the void was stale, still, undisturbed for decades.

Inside, nestled within the cool darkness, wrapped carefully in yellowed, brittle linen, was a bundle she hadn't seen before. It was smaller than the previous box of letters she'd found under the floorboard in the bedroom. Softer. Almost delicate. It spoke of tenderness, of careful preservation.

She hesitated, her breath caught in her throat, the thumping of her heart now loud in her ears. Then, with a trembling hand, she reached in and gently unwrapped the cloth.

A single, sealed envelope lay on top, its paper thick and uncreased.

Beneath it, nestled within the soft folds of linen, were two tiny objects: a pair of baby booties.

They were hand-stitched, a pale, faded blue, the wool thinned and slightly misshapen with time, imbued with an ethereal fragility. They looked like they'd been handled many times, cherished and mourned, perhaps once tucked away quickly, urgently, with trembling hands, in a moment of desperate concealment. They were impossibly small, miniature versions of something designed for warmth and comfort, now silent witnesses to a life that might have been.

Sophie stared at them, the miniature size bringing a sudden, sharp pain to her chest. The truth they hinted at was stark, undeniable.

The envelope was heavier than it looked, containing more than just a single sheet of paper. She turned it over, her fingers tracing its unmarked surface.

There was no address. No stamp. No formal closing. Just a name, written in Elsie's unmistakable, faded ink, in a slightly larger, more deliberate hand than the letters:

"For when the time is right."

Her breath caught, a small, choked gasp. The words, simple yet profoundly resonant, hung in the quiet air, a message from the past, a silent instruction from Elsie to a future recipient.

She swallowed, her throat dry, the enormity of the discovery pressing down on her. The tiny booties weighed almost nothing in her hand, their lightness a stark contrast to the immense weight of the truth they hinted at. Elsie had had a child. A child she had hidden. A child whose existence was a secret buried within these very walls, alongside the letters of a man who loved her deeply.

She didn't open the envelope.

Not yet. The impulse to know, to tear it open and devour its contents, was almost unbearable, but something held her back. A profound sense of Elsie's privacy, of the sacred nature of this particular secret, perhaps. Or perhaps, a fear of what else the envelope might contain, what further depths of grief or complication it might reveal. Her own grief, a heavy stone, still sat in her chest, and she knew, instinctively, that this revelation required a clearer mind, a stronger heart.

Instead, she sat back on her heels, the floorboards cold beneath her, and held the tiny booties in her palm. Their softness, their delicate craftsmanship, spoke of a mother's love, of hopes and dreams woven into threads of wool.

They didn't belong to her, not literally, not physically. But they did. Somehow. A profound, undeniable connection, a thread of blood and history, stretched from Elsie, to the unknown child, to Sophie herself.

The truth was stretching toward her now, not just a hint, but a palpable presence, just out of reach, but she could feel its shape forming, solidifying in her mind. The implications of this hidden child, born in the midst of war, unacknowledged, unmentioned, were vast.

She glanced toward the cold fireplace, toward the quiet stack of Elsie's letters, their secrets slowly unfolding. One life layered over another. Elsie's story, now inextricably linked to her own. One generation whispering to the next, secrets passed down through hidden panels and unspoken truths. The cottage, once a quiet refuge, now felt like a living archive, breathing with the hidden lives that had unfolded within its walls.

The silence of the cottage settled around her again, no longer quite so still. It felt charged, imbued with memory, with life, with sorrow, and with the immense, unspoken legacy of a secret that had finally, patiently, chosen its moment to reveal itself. The grieving daughter, unknowingly, had become the keeper of a profound family truth.

# Chapter Twelve

Lincolnshire, January 1942

Every morning, the ritual was the same, a desperate, silent prayer against the growing void. Elsie would wake, usually before dawn, with a sense of urgent dread. She would wrap herself tightly in her thick wool coat, its rough fabric a small shield against the penetrating chill, tug on her heavy, mud-stained boots, and crunch across the icy path that led from her cottage doorstep to the well. Her gaze, raw with unspoken hope and a crushing disappointment, swept across the frozen ground, searching the bleak expanse before the sun had fully lifted the long, skeletal shadows from the orchard trees. Each time, she hoped against hope to find a new, precious envelope tucked between the coal bucket and the doorframe, or slipped under the rough welcome mat by some kind, understanding postman who knew her name, knew her desperate longing.

But there was nothing. Never anything. No new letter. No sign of Thomas. The cold, unyielding silence from him was a constant, gnawing presence. The last words she'd received from him—hurried, full of longing, a desperate promise of return—now felt like they were written a lifetime ago, a relic from a different, less terrifying reality. She kept reading them over, running her fingers across the faded ink, hoping to pull something new from the spaces between the lines, a hidden hint, a secret promise. But they only grew quieter with each passing day, their words fading not just in ink, but in the certainty they once held.

The silence pressed in, heavy and constant, filling the cottage, filling her days, louder than any sound. It was the silence of absence, of unanswered questions, of a future rapidly shrinking into a terrifying, solitary present.

She didn't write back that week. Not yet. Her body, with its insistent, alarming changes, had other, more pressing plans for her. The words she needed to write, the truths she had to put to paper, felt too vast, too terrifying to articulate.

The sickness had worsened, becoming a relentless, debilitating companion. What had once been occasional morning nausea, a transient queasiness she could attribute to cold or stress, was now a daily, unpredictable onslaught. It struck at any hour, with brutal suddenness, twisting her stomach into a tight, rebellious knot. She often found herself crouched behind the barn, or hidden in the furthest reaches of the tool shed, forehead pressed against the rough, cold stone of the walls, her breath coming in ragged gasps, waiting for the wave of nausea to pass, for the churning in her gut to ease. Her energy, once robust despite the demanding farm work, had dwindled to a fragile flicker, leaving her constantly, profoundly weary. Even the orchard, her sacred, secret space, the place of their love and whispered promises, had started to feel too far away, too distant to reach when the nausea hit.

She tried desperately to hide it, retreating further into herself, her usual quietness becoming an almost impenetrable barrier. But Gladys, with her youthful exuberance and surprisingly keen eye, noticed.

"You've gone white again, Elsie," the girl said one afternoon, her bright, innocent gaze fixed on Elsie's pale face as they mucked out the henhouse, the air thick with the acrid smell of manure and damp straw. Her voice was tinged with genuine concern.

"It's the cold," Elsie replied quickly, her voice sharp with defensive reflex, a desperate attempt to bat away the intrusion.

Gladys, however, was not so easily dismissed. She leaned against a support beam, her small frame surprisingly steady. "Cold doesn't make your knees buckle, Elsie," she observed, her tone gentle but firm. "I saw you earlier, nearly went down by the pump."

"I'm fine," Elsie insisted, turning away, pretending to adjust a loose board in the chicken coop, her hands trembling slightly despite her efforts to control them.

But she wasn't. And the truth, a quiet, inexorable force, was slowly, unstoppably, revealing itself. When Margaret, with her usual brisk efficiency, called her in early from the fields one particularly bitter morning, her face etched with a rare concern, handing her a steaming mug of weak, almost tasteless tea and telling her, simply, to sit, Elsie didn't argue. She sank onto the wooden stool by the fire, her body suddenly heavy, utterly devoid of the strength to resist.

"I'm not daft, Elsie," Margaret said, her voice gruff but not unkind, her gaze direct and unflinching. Her eyes, usually so focused on tasks, now studied Elsie's face with a quiet intensity. "You've lost weight, even with all the food. And you've gone quiet. Quieter than even your usual quiet. That girl Gladys, bless her busy tongue, says you're being sick in the mornings. Says you're looking a bit green around the gills."

Elsie stared into the mug, its tepid warmth doing little to penetrate the chill that had settled in her bones. The truth, now spoken aloud, hung in the air between them, vast and unyielding. She didn't know what to say, how to begin to articulate the terrifying, incredible secret that had consumed her. The words felt too big, too fraught with consequence.

Margaret didn't wait for her to speak. Her face, usually a mask of granite resolve, softened imperceptibly. "If you're not ill with the grippe, then it's something else, isn't it? And Elsie, I don't need to know who he is, or if he's still out there, or anything else about your private business. But I need to know if you're going to need help. If this farm needs to make arrangements. We're at war, girl, but we're not savages. We look after our own, especially when times get hard."

Elsie looked up, her eyes, wide and filled with unshed tears, meeting Margaret's steady gaze. The kindness in Margaret's voice, the unexpected understanding, was a sudden, overwhelming balm. The words she had suppressed for weeks, the truth she had guarded so fiercely, now struggled to find release. "I think... yes. I think I might," she managed, her voice barely a whisper, thick with emotion.

That was all she could say. The words felt too big to speak aloud, even now, too immense for the confines of the small cottage. But it was enough. It was an acknowledgement, a desperate plea, a quiet surrender to an undeniable reality.

Margaret nodded, a slow, deliberate movement, her expression softening further, devoid of judgment. "Then we'll manage, Elsie. We always do." Her voice was low, resolute, a promise etched in the gruff kindness. It was not a guarantee of ease, but a quiet assurance of support.

The Promise Beneath the Skin
The next day, Elsie walked to the orchard, driven by an urgent, almost primal need to be in their place, to confront the silent trees with her profound, terrifying truth. The sky was iron-grey above her, a vast, oppressive canvas. The cold bit into her fingers through her worn gloves, numbing the tips, yet she welcomed the sharp sensation, anything to cut through the swirling chaos in her mind. She walked directly to the gnarled central tree, their tree, the ancient sentinel that had witnessed their secret love, and stood beneath its bare, skeletal branches. She looked at the place where Thomas had stood last, where he had pulled her close, where he had kissed her with a deep, certain tenderness. She remembered the low stone wall where he had held her, wrapped her in his arms like he would never let her go, his body a solid anchor against the shifting world.

She placed a trembling hand on her stomach. It was still flat, still easily hidden under layers of thick wool and the carefully constructed silence she had maintained. But the weight of the truth had settled there, a new, undeniable presence, pulsing quietly like a second heartbeat, small yet insistent. It was a warmth, a pressure, a profound, undeniable reality.

She was carrying his child.

The knowledge, once a distant, terrifying possibility, was now a vivid, undeniable truth. It was his child, a living, breathing testament to their love, a tiny, vulnerable part of Thomas still connected to her, to this world. She thought of the locket he had taken with him, a sliver of her image pressed against his heart, a silent promise of home. The handkerchief he had given her still lay under her pillow, worn and soft, but she hadn't touched it in days. It felt too tender, too intimate, too fraught with the bitter irony of his absence.

Her life was changing, irrevocably, profoundly. And he wasn't here. He was out there, somewhere in the terrifying, chaotic churn of the war, perhaps already a ghost. The fear for him, the profound longing for his return, now mingled with a fierce, protective instinct for the tiny life growing within her.

That evening, the cottage felt both profoundly quiet and utterly changed. The air was thick with the weight of her unspoken truth. She sat by the fire for a long while, watching the flames dance, gathering the immense strength it took to put words to paper, to articulate the unspeakable. The pen trembled slightly in her hand, not from the physical chill of the room, but from the sheer enormity of what she was about to commit to paper, a secret that would bind her forever.

"My Dearest Thomas," she wrote, her hand slow, deliberate, each word chosen with a new, profound care. "There is so much I don't know how to say. So many truths that cannot travel across the sea, across the battlefields. I waited for another letter. I still wait every morning, my heart aching with expectation. But none have come. The silence from you is a heavy thing, Thomas. I hope you are safe. I hope you are somewhere with trees, somewhere that reminds you of peace, of home. I hope the locket I gave you still brings you stillness in the chaos."

"The orchard is bare now, Thomas. Stripped of its leaves, stark against the winter sky. Quiet, profoundly quiet. But something grows here. Quietly. Secretly. A new life. Your life. Our life. I don't know what it will mean, or where it will take me, this profound change, this immense responsibility, but I know, with every fibre of my being, that it started with you. With us. In our orchard, under the last light of summer."

"If you come back to me, Thomas, there will be more than just my arms waiting. There will be a small, precious part of you here, a living, breathing testament to our love. A child. Our child."

"Yours always, Elsie"

She folded the letter carefully, her movements precise, almost reverent, as if the paper held the fragile essence of her hope. She tied it with a fresh, crisp length of ribbon, its colour a vibrant red against the pale paper, a defiant splash of life. Then she knelt to place it under the same loose floorboard, resting it gently among the others, a new, profound addition to the hidden chronicle of her life. The fire in the hearth had burned low, its embers glowing softly, a dying heart in the vast quiet. Outside, the wind rattled the shutters, a mournful lament against the old cottage walls.

She rose and wrapped herself in a thick wool blanket, the familiar weight a small comfort, carrying a cup of weak, now cold tea to the window. The orchard was still visible in the moonlight, a ghostly landscape, the frost silvering the grass and the lower branches, turning the bare trees into shimmering, ethereal sculptures. She imagined Thomas walking through it again, his coat brushing the brittle leaves, his hands reaching for her, his eyes full of the promise of return, as if no time had passed, no war had intervened.

The cottage creaked around her, old and worn and full of silence. But it was a comforting kind of quiet now—the kind that made room for thoughts to stretch, for new realities to take root. It was no longer the silence of absence, but the quiet of profound change, of deep, quiet understanding.

She thought of her parents. What would they say? The judgment. The shame. The impossibility of explaining Thomas, the war, the circumstances. She hadn't written to them in weeks, the distance growing between them, unsure how to begin to explain the life she now lived, the profound secret she carried. How could she begin to tell them about Thomas, a man who might be gone forever? About the child, a living consequence of a love they would never understand?

She had considered leaving. Taking a train somewhere, anywhere, and starting fresh in a city where no one knew her name, where her past could be shed like an old skin. But the orchard rooted her, its gnarled branches reaching deep into the earth, holding her fast. The letters, the hidden chronicle of her love, grounded her. The idea of him—of them—was not something she could leave behind. This was her home now. This was where she would wait.

Margaret had said they would manage. And for the first time, Elsie felt a flicker of belief in that gruff promise. But she knew the weeks ahead would be long. Her body would change, visibly so. Whispers would inevitably start in the small village. The war wouldn't wait for her to find her footing, wouldn't pause for her private revolution.

Still, she stayed by the window until her tea went cold, until the moonlight faded and the first faint streaks of dawn appeared on the horizon. She watched the orchard, a silent sentinel of her love and her profound new reality. And somewhere in the dark, into the vast, indifferent expanse of the night, she whispered a promise to the wind, a vow whispered not just for herself, but for the tiny, precious life within her:

"I'll raise this child with love. Fierce, unwavering love. Even if I have to do it alone. Even if you never come back."

And somewhere in the vast, cold dark, the silence seemed to shift, as if the very air acknowledged her vow, absorbing it into the timeless fabric of the land.

# Chapter Thirteen

The morning sun filtered tentatively through the kitchen window, struggling to pierce the persistent grey of the sky, throwing pale, ethereal stripes across the worn floorboards. Sophie sat at the table, a forgotten cup of tea cooling between her hands, its surface reflecting the dull light. The house was profoundly still, save for the occasional, comforting creak of settling timber, a sigh from the ancient structure, or the soft, whispering rustle of wind against the windowpanes. It had been three days, three long, quiet days, since she'd returned from her father's funeral, a period of numb introspection. The acute, sharp edge of grief, that initial, searing wound, was no longer raw, but had settled into a dull, constant ache, like a low, persistent hum in the background of everything she did, a quiet, mournful soundtrack to her solitary existence.

She hadn't told her mother about the sealed envelope, or the tiny, fragile baby booties she'd found hidden in the wall panel. There hadn't been a moment for it, not amidst the somber preparations, the hushed condolences, the overwhelming weight of immediate loss. And now, the opportune moment had passed, slipping away like a silent current. Even thinking about it, about the truth those objects hinted at, felt like stepping too close to the edge of something immense, something she didn't yet want to fully see, to acknowledge. It was a secret too profound, too potentially shattering, to share when her mother was already so utterly broken.

She looked down at the sealed envelope that lay on the table beside her cooling tea, its thick, quality paper a stark contrast to the rough kitchen wood. The handwriting was elegant, old-fashioned, unmistakably Elsie's. For when the time is right. Those words, written with such deliberate care, had been a silent companion for days. She'd stared at them every night before bed, traced the delicate loops of the script, touched the crisp edge of the paper, debated, for long, agonizing moments, whether to open it, to unleash the secrets it held. Each time, fear, or perhaps a lingering reverence for Elsie's privacy, had made her slip it back into the drawer beside her bed.

Today, however, something felt different. The air in the cottage, usually still and contemplative, felt charged with a subtle, insistent energy, urging her forward. The weight of Elsie's untold story, and the growing sense of its connection to her own life, had become too heavy to ignore.

She reached for it, her hand moving with a slow, deliberate purpose. Her hands were steady, miraculously so, but her chest tightened, a cold, constricting band of anticipation. She slid her thumb carefully under the aged wax seal, the resistance giving way with a soft, almost mournful sigh of splitting paper. Inside was a single sheet, folded precisely into thirds, its edges crisp despite the years.

Before she could fully unfold it, before she could even glimpse the first line of text, she stopped.

A sudden rush of emotion, thick and overwhelming, crept up her throat, choking her. It wasn't just fear, or even curiosity. It was a profound sense of connection, a sudden, vivid image of Elsie herself. She stood abruptly, moving instinctively to the window, the still-folded letter clutched tightly in her hand, her knuckles white. Outside, the orchard stood bare and silent, its gnarled branches reaching like skeletal fingers towards the grey sky, still silvered with the last vestiges of frost from the dawn. The trees looked like something from another world, ancient sentinels, still and frozen in time, holding their breath through countless winters. She imagined Elsie, her mysterious great-aunt, standing there all those years ago—her back perhaps to these very same windows, her heart aching, waiting for a letter that never came, for a man who never returned, carrying a secret that would define her life.

She blinked hard, forcing back the sudden sting of tears, her vision momentarily blurred. She took a ragged breath and turned back to the kitchen table, the light from the window falling full on her face.

She couldn't read it alone. Not yet. The weight of it, the profound implications, felt too immense to bear in solitary silence.

Instead, she sat down, pushing the tea mug aside, and opened her laptop. She stared at the screen for a moment, the cursor blinking, waiting for her command, then typed out a short email, her fingers moving with a new, decisive purpose.

Hi Ben,

I found something else. Something... significant. A letter. Hidden behind a panel in the sitting room. It was with a pair of baby booties.

I haven't read it yet. But I think it connects everything. I think it explains Elsie's silence.

I could use your help. Not just with the research. With this.

-Sophie

She hit send before she could second-guess herself, before the lingering doubts could creep in. The email vanished, a message launched into the unknown, carrying the burden of Elsie's profound secret, and Sophie's own growing sense of being inextricably caught in its web.

## The Unveiling

Then, finally, after the email was sent, after the point of no return, she opened the letter. Slowly, meticulously. The paper unfolded with a soft rustle, revealing Elsie's familiar, elegant handwriting, now seeming to pulse with a new, urgent significance.

The first line, stark and immediate, leaped from the page, a direct address from across the decades:

"I never wanted this to be a secret."

Sophie felt her heart catch in her throat, a sharp, painful constriction. The simple, honest declaration was a key, unlocking something fundamental about Elsie, about her life, about the profound burden she had carried. It was a quiet confession that resonated with Sophie's own unspoken thoughts about secrets, about the heavy cost of silence.

She kept reading, her eyes devouring the words, a silent witness to Elsie's posthumous confession. The rest of the letter lay flat in her lap, the words swimming slightly through the sudden, fresh blur of tears that stung her eyes. She hadn't cried during her father's funeral, not properly, not when she stood at his bedside, dry-eyed and numb. But now, as Elsie's carefully chosen words, filled with raw honesty and profound regret, spilled across the page, something deep inside Sophie cracked.

It wasn't just sadness that overwhelmed her. It was the recognition of something larger, something ancient and deeply human. It was the weight of legacy, the bitter sting of regret, the echoing sorrow of lives unlived, of choices forced, of truths unspoken. It was a testament to the enduring power of love, even in absence, and the profound, often tragic, consequences of war.

Sophie stood again, moving instinctively to the window, the letter now clutched tightly in her hand, its truths vibrating through her. She opened it once more, the crumpled paper flattening under her trembling fingers, and read it from the very beginning, letting each word sink into her consciousness, resonate with her own burgeoning understanding.

"I never wanted this to be a secret. Never desired to live a life shadowed by what could not be spoken. But some choices, once made, under impossible circumstances, cast long shadows. I have carried this one alone for most of my life, a heavy burden that shaped every path I took, every silence I kept."

"If you are reading this, then the time I feared, and yet hoped for, has come. The time when this truth, this life, must be acknowledged. Someone I loved with a fierce, unwavering devotion was taken from me before I had the chance to tell him the truth, the most profound truth that linked us. And I lost the chance to tell the child we created together the full story of his father. The world, in its cruel wisdom, denied me that."

"I hope you will understand, whoever you are, why I kept this buried. I hope you will understand the impossible choices of a woman alone, in a world at war, with a secret too vast to share. I hope you will forgive me for the silence, for the years of omission. It was a silence born of love, and of fear."

Sophie sat again, this time sinking slowly onto the cold floor beside the fireplace, Elsie's words ringing in her ears, her mind reeling. The baby booties, small and impossibly fragile, were still tucked into the corner of the yellowed linen bundle. She picked one up, turning it over and over in her hand, feeling the thin, worn wool against her skin.

Elsie had never spoken of a child. Not to anyone, as far as Sophie could tell from her father's guarded reticence or Marjorie's knowing silences. And yet, this letter wasn't written to a stranger. It wasn't vague or hypothetical, a general confession to the future. It was written for someone real, someone specific. A direct address from a mother to her hidden child, or to that child's direct descendant.

And that someone, Sophie suspected with a chilling certainty that settled deep in her bones, had no idea. That someone was her father. The father she had just buried. The quiet, stoic man who had taught her how to change a tyre, who had loved her in his own complicated way, had carried within him a secret lineage, a truth that had been buried even deeper than Elsie's letters.

She picked up the letter again, her hands shaking now, reading further, desperate for more details, for names, for confirmation.

"I was very young when it happened. And he, Thomas, was taken before he ever knew. Before I could find the words, before I could reach him. It wasn't meant to be this way, this solitary path. I wanted to give him something beautiful to return to, a new life, a family. But the war stole that chance from both of us, from our fragile hope. It stole him. And it stole the open, proud acknowledgment of our child."

"I named him. Just once, in my head, in the quiet of the night, when no one else could hear. A secret name, a whisper of love. I saw his face in dreams, a blend of Thomas and myself. And then, for his safety, for his future, for the impossible circumstances of our time, I had to let him go. I had to let him go out into the world, to a different life, knowing he would never know the full truth of his beginning. It was the hardest thing I have ever done."

Sophie wiped her eyes with the sleeve of her jumper, the fabric damp and rough against her wet cheeks. Elsie's pain, her unimaginable sacrifice, poured from the page, a raw, unvarnished testament to a love that demanded an impossible choice. She imagined Elsie writing this in the dim light of the cottage, not just years, but perhaps decades— decades—after the war had ended, after her child was grown, after her love was a distant echo. She pictured Elsie pausing between sentences, pen hovering, unsure whether to keep going, unsure who would ever read it, or if it would simply remain buried, another secret. The enduring weight of that solitary burden was crushing.

A sudden, sharp ping from her laptop jolted her from her trance. Ben's name flashed in her inbox, a beacon from the present.

On my way. – Ben

She didn't reply. She simply set the letter back on the table, carefully smoothing its creases, a sacred document. She moved slowly to the armchair by the fire, sinking into its worn comfort, and waited. Waited for Ben, for the next step, for the moment she would have to speak this impossible truth aloud.

The frost outside was beginning to melt, relinquishing its bitter grip. Somewhere in the orchard, beneath the still-bare branches, the first imperceptible signs of spring were stirring, a quiet promise of new life, of renewal, even after the longest, coldest winter. And inside the cottage, a new truth, born of old secrets, was finally, irrevocably, coming to light.

# Chapter Fourteen

This chapter shifts the narrative into active investigation with Ben's assistance, and significantly deepens the emotional stakes for Sophie, connecting Elsie's secret directly to her recent grief. I will expand it to over 3000 words by intensifying Sophie's initial state of grief and numbness, detailing the emotional weight of showing Ben the discoveries, elaborating on their discussion, and emphasizing the development of their partnership and Sophie's renewed sense of purpose. The core plot points will remain unchanged.

Chapter 14: A Shared Burden
Sophie heard the knock just after noon, a firm, yet hesitant rap that startled her from her introspective quiet. She hadn't realised how long she'd been sitting there, curled in the armchair by the fire, its embers now fading to a dull glow. A thick, wool blanket was still wrapped tightly around her shoulders, a flimsy shield against the pervasive chill that had seeped back into the cottage. The remnants of cold tea sat forgotten on the small side table beside her, its surface ringed with a faint condensation mark. She had been lost in thought, adrift in the silent aftermath of her father's funeral, the weight of Elsie's newly discovered secret pressing down on her.

She rose slowly, feeling the stiffness in her limbs, and opened the door to find Ben standing on the doorstep. He was bundled in a thick navy overcoat and a practical, dark scarf, his glasses fogging slightly from the stark difference between the cold outside air and the marginally warmer interior of the cottage. He offered a small, polite smile that quickly faded, dissolving into an expression of concern as his perceptive grey eyes took in the lingering grief and exhaustion etched on her face.

"You okay, Sophie?" he asked, his voice low and genuinely sympathetic, his gaze direct.

Sophie stepped back and nodded, a slight, almost imperceptible movement of her head. "Come in, Ben. It's... it's cold out here." Her voice was a little rough, unused after hours of silence.

He entered, carefully removing his scarf, brushing a few stray snowflakes—light, gentle flurries that had started to fall—from the dark wool of his coat. He closed the door quietly behind him, sealing out the damp, cold world. She led him into the kitchen, the warmest room in the cottage, where the sealed envelope, the now-opened letter, and the tiny baby booties still lay on the table, stark against the worn wooden surface, awaiting his inspection.

"I got your email, Sophie," Ben said softly, his voice respectful, tinged with a quiet understanding. He pulled out one of the kitchen chairs, its wood groaning faintly in protest, and sat down opposite her, his gaze immediately falling to the items on the table. "You said you found a letter? And... something more?"

Sophie sat opposite him, her hands clasped tightly in her lap, her gaze fixed on the objects between them. "Yes. A letter. And more than that." Her voice was barely a whisper, the enormity of the revelation still overwhelming.

She reached out and, with a gentle, almost reverent touch, unwrapped the baby booties from their yellowed linen shroud, carefully laying them beside the open letter. The soft, faded blue wool seemed to glow faintly in the subdued light.

Ben stared at them for a long moment, his expression unreadable. Then, slowly, with a careful, almost tender movement, he picked one up. He turned the impossibly tiny bootie over in his large hand, his thumb tracing the delicate, hand-stitched pattern. "These are old," he murmured, his voice hushed. "Handmade. Exquisite."

"They were wrapped with the letter, hidden behind a panel near the fireplace in the sitting room," Sophie explained, her voice gaining a little strength, a sense of purpose returning to her. "Elsie must've hidden them there. Deliberately."

Ben glanced from the bootie to her face, his gaze questioning. "And the letter? The one you mentioned in your email?"

Sophie hesitated for a beat, a final, fleeting surge of protective instinct for Elsie's privacy. Then, with a decisive movement, she pushed the unfolded letter, Elsie's last, profound confession, across the table towards him. "It's... a confession, of sorts. From my great-aunt Elsie. She had a child. During the war. A son."

Ben's eyes widened slightly as he picked up the letter, his brow furrowing as he began to scan the first few lines, Elsie's unequivocal declaration: "I never wanted this to be a secret." He read quickly, his gaze sweeping across the page, absorbing the essence of her desperate words. Then he looked up, his grey eyes meeting Sophie's, now filled with a deep understanding. "Does it say what happened to the child? If he survived?"

"She had to give him up," Sophie said, her voice strained, a raw ache in her throat. "That's all she says. That she had to let him go for his safety, for his future. For the impossible circumstances of the time."

He sat back slowly, absorbing the information, his initial professional detachment replaced by a profound empathy. He looked from the letter, to the tiny booties, to Sophie's grief-stricken face. "So Thomas...?"

Sophie nodded, confirming the unspoken. "The father." The word hung in the air between them, loaded with implications.

Ben was quiet for a long moment, the only sound the soft crackle of the fire and the gentle falling of snow outside. His gaze drifted to the window, lost in contemplation. Then, gently, respectfully, he asked the question that had been haunting Sophie since the discovery. "Do you think your dad knew, Sophie? About this? About Elsie having a child?"

Sophie's lips parted, but no words came, caught in the sudden surge of overwhelming emotion. The very thought of her stoic, reserved father carrying such a profound, unacknowledged truth was almost unbearable. She stood abruptly, unable to remain seated under the weight of the question, and crossed to the kitchen window, wrapping her arms tightly around herself, staring out at the silent, snow-covered orchard.

"He didn't," she said at last, her voice raw, imbued with a fierce certainty that stemmed from instinct rather than concrete proof. "He couldn't have. He wouldn't have kept it from me. Not like this. And he certainly wouldn't have kept it from Mum. He wouldn't have carried such a burden alone."

Ben tilted his head, his gaze following her, his expression a blend of understanding and professional curiosity. "What makes you so sure, Sophie?"

"Because he died last week," she said, her voice breaking, the words tumbling out, sharp and sudden, despite her efforts to maintain composure. "He collapsed suddenly. A heart attack. I... I was driving up here when it happened. I didn't get there in time to say goodbye."

Ben's eyes widened, a flicker of genuine shock crossing his face. He pushed his glasses up his nose, running a hand through his already messy hair. "Sophie—God, I'm so incredibly sorry. I had no idea. There was no mention in your emails, of course. I... I'm truly sorry for your loss." His voice was gentle, deeply sympathetic.

She shook her head quickly, dismissing his apologies. The knowledge of his kindness, his immediate empathy, was a unexpected comfort. "It's okay, Ben. You couldn't have known. I didn't tell anyone. I couldn't. It was... too much."

Ben stood slowly, deliberately, and crossed the room, stopping a respectful distance from her. "Do you want to talk about it, Sophie? You don't have to. But I'm here if you do."

She turned to face him, her eyes, red-rimmed and aching, meeting his. "I'm not sure what there is to say, honestly. He collapsed suddenly. Heart attack. It was quick, they said. But... I didn't get there in time. That's the part that sticks. The regret."

Ben was quiet, his presence a steady, solid anchor in her storm of grief. He didn't offer platitudes or empty reassurances. He simply listened, respectful, empathetic. She was profoundly grateful for that.

"I haven't told my mum about this," she added, gesturing vaguely back towards the table, towards Elsie's letter and the booties. "It felt... too much. Too close to her own grief. To her own world crumbling. I can't add this to her burden, not now."

He nodded, understanding immediately. "That makes perfect sense. Do you think you will, eventually?"

"Eventually, yes. I have to. But I just need to understand it first. I need to understand Elsie's choices. And I need to know... what happened to him."

They sat in silence for a while then, the unspoken weight of both their lives and Elsie's history filling the room. The fire crackled softly in the hearth, its warmth a tangible comfort. Outside, snow began to fall again in light, gentle flurries, drifting past the window like tiny, ethereal dancers.

Ben leaned forward, his voice a quiet, compassionate question. "Would you like help finding out what happened to the baby, Sophie? The child Elsie had to give up? His name, his fate?"

Sophie looked at him, her gaze direct, unwavering, a new resolve hardening her features. "Can we, Ben? Is it even possible? I don't even know where to start looking for something like that. All the records were so... vague."

He smiled, a gentle, reassuring expression. "You've already started, Sophie. You've done the hardest part. Between the hospital record, the physical proof of the booties, and this letter, Elsie's own words—we've got something concrete to go on. More than most people ever find."

She gave a small, tired laugh, a raw sound of incredulity and unexpected lightness. "We?"

Ben met her gaze, his expression serious, steady. "Yes, Sophie. We. You're not alone in this. Not anymore."

She blinked rapidly, tears blurring her vision, and nodded, swallowing the thick lump that had formed in her throat. The offer of shared burden, of shared purpose, was an unexpected gift, a lifeline.

"I could start by checking parish records from that period, looking for births to 'E. Hale' or similar, perhaps even searching for any local mother-and-baby homes that operated in Lincolnshire during wartime," he continued, his mind already shifting into professional gear. "And any adoption services that might have been active. It will be a painstaking search, but there might be a lead, however faint."

Sophie stared at Elsie's letter again, its last line resonating with a new, profound meaning. "I want to find him, Ben. Whoever he was. Whoever he became." The words were a quiet vow, a promise to Elsie, and perhaps, to her father.

Ben stood, his movements purposeful. "Then let's start. We have a good chance, I think." He reached into the inner pocket of his navy overcoat and pulled out a small, well-worn notebook and a pencil. "I'll make a few calls this afternoon.

There's a local historian I know, a retired archivist who's spent decades cataloguing wartime family separations, children displaced or given up. He might know exactly where to look for this kind of information, or at least point us in the right direction."

"Thank you, Ben," she said softly, her voice thick with gratitude.

Ben smiled again, this time more warmly, his grey eyes alight with a shared sense of purpose. "I'll be in touch soon. With anything I find."

As he turned to leave, he paused at the door, his hand on the cold metal knob. "If you need anything else, Sophie," he added, his voice gentle, "anything at all. Even just a terrible cup of tea and a chat. Or if the grief becomes too much. I'm around."

She managed a gentle, almost genuine laugh, a fragile sound that broke the solemnity of the moment. "I'll keep that in mind, Ben. Thank you."

After he left, the door clicking softly shut behind him, the cottage settled once more into its quiet. Sophie sat down again at the table, her gaze falling to the tiny booties. She picked them up, holding them carefully in her hands, feeling their lightness, their profound weight.

The frost outside, she noticed, had finally melted, leaving only dampness behind. But something inside her felt clearer now, lighter, despite the sorrow.

Stronger.

She was ready. Ready to find out the rest of Elsie's story. Ready to uncover the truth of the hidden child. And perhaps, in doing so, to finally understand the complex, unspoken narrative of her own family.

# Chapter Fifteen

Every morning, the ritual of hope and disappointment was meticulously observed. Elsie stood at the window of the cottage, a solitary figure framed against the cold, grey light, watching snowflakes fall softly and silently against the gnarled, ancient limbs of the orchard trees. The branches, now stripped bare by the relentless winter, looked like brittle, skeletal fingers, webbing against the bruised, heavy sky like fragile, intricate veins. She placed a gloved hand against the cold, unyielding glass, its icy touch a small, sharp reminder of the world outside. She hoped, without any real expectation left, for a fleeting glimpse of the postman, a solitary silhouette trudging up the long, muddy track, a harbinger of news, of life from beyond the horizon.

But there was nothing. Never anything. The post, once a daily lifeline, had not come for weeks, for what felt like an eternity. No more letters from Thomas. No more impossible hope that his familiar handwriting might appear, like a miraculous apparition, in her hands. The last one she'd received—that brief, desperate, treasured message, now carefully tucked inside her pillowcase, a fragile comfort against the chill of the night—was fading from her mind as surely as its ink was fading from the page. Its words, once so vibrant, were now echoes, growing fainter with each passing day, losing their sharp edges, blurring into the vast, silent tapestry of absence.

She still wrote. Sometimes short, frantic notes, quick bursts of longing and fear. Sometimes pages, filled with the mundane details of farm life interwoven with her deepest, most guarded confessions. She folded them meticulously, tied them with fresh lengths of ribbon, and added them, one by one, to the hollow under the floorboard in her bedroom. It was a growing archive of words Thomas would likely never read, a testament to a love suspended in time, a desperate attempt to anchor him, and herself, to a forgotten promise.

Her belly had begun to round, subtly at first, a gentle, almost imperceptible curve beneath her thick layers of clothing. Not noticeably to others, not yet, she hoped. But to her, every curve, every new ache, every subtle shift within her body whispered incessantly of what was to come, a relentless, undeniable countdown. The nausea, once a violent daily torment, had lessened, replaced by a deeper, quieter, more profound discomfort. Her back ached constantly, a dull, persistent throb that never truly eased. Her legs tired quickly, growing heavy and leaden with even the shortest walks. And though Margaret had said little more since that quiet, knowing conversation in January, Elsie could feel the farmer's gaze on her, watching her more closely now, her sharp eyes missing nothing, even when her face remained impassive.

Gladys, too, had changed. The girl was less chirpy, her endless, tuneless whistling replaced by stretches of uncharacteristic quiet. Her bright-eyed optimism seemed to have dimmed, a subtle cloud passing over her youthful countenance. Elsie caught her staring now and then, her gaze lingering, curious, tinged with an unspoken concern. One afternoon, while collecting eggs, their hands brushing in the straw-filled nest boxes, Gladys had opened her mouth as though to speak—her lips forming a tentative question— then, thinking better of it, her gaze had dropped, and she had turned abruptly away, leaving the words unsaid, the question hanging in the air.

Elsie wasn't angry at Gladys's observation, or even at Margaret's watchful silence. She understood. She'd have stared, too. The physical changes, however subtle, were undeniable to a knowing eye. The retreat into herself was a natural defence, a means to protect the growing life within her, to shield her vulnerability from a world that had no mercy for such complexities.

She tried to keep working, to maintain the demanding pace of farm life, but the effort grew harder, more exhausting with each passing day. The heavy lifting she avoided, feigning stiffness or a twisted ankle. The walks to the far fields, once a solitary escape, became shorter, more arduous. She stayed closer to the cottage now, lingering in the comforting warmth of the sputtering fire, finding solace in the rhythmic crackle of the flames and the unspoken words of the letters she hadn't yet written, the ones that formed in her mind, waiting for the quiet of night.

Margaret's Ultimatum

One evening, just after supper, when the last light had faded from the sky and the cold had deepened its grip on the land, Margaret knocked on the cottage door. Her knock was firm, deliberate, not the casual rap of a neighbour dropping by. Elsie opened it slowly, her heart thudding, unsure of what to expect, a premonition of finality settling over her.

"You've got a decision to make, Elsie," Margaret said without preamble, her voice as blunt and unyielding as the frozen earth outside, yet laced with a weary kindness. She stood framed in the doorway, her silhouette dark against the fading light, her expression unreadable. "You can stay here through it, and I'll do what I can, mind you. But it's not the place for a birth. Not here. There are no proper facilities, no one trained for such things. And once folk start talking, Elsie, once the whispers begin to spread through the village, I can't unhear them. And I can't protect you from them."

Elsie nodded, her throat tight, a suffocating knot of fear and resignation. She knew. She had known this conversation was coming, had seen it approaching with the rounding of her belly, the increasing fatigue. She stared at Margaret, her own eyes pleading for understanding, for a way out that didn't exist.

"There's a place in Lincoln," Margaret continued, her voice softening slightly, though her gaze remained firm. "A quiet home. Run by the Sisters. They take girls like you, see you through the confinement. No questions asked, no judgments. Discretion is their watchword. They help with the arrangements afterwards, if that's what you decide. It's for the best, Elsie. For you, and for the child."

Elsie's breath hitched. "Will they make me give the baby up, Margaret?" The question was raw, desperate, the fear of losing this precious, impossible life consuming her.

"They'll make it seem like it's your idea," Margaret said, her voice still without malice, but imbued with the hard-won wisdom of a woman who understood the cruel realities of the world. "That's how these things go, Elsie. For a girl in your situation, with no husband, no support, and a war on... it's the usual path. The only path, often." She paused, her gaze steady. "It's safer for the child, too. A fresh start. A chance at a proper life, without the stigma."

Elsie felt a rush of hot tears behind her eyes, a sharp sting of pain and indignation, but she held her expression perfectly still, a mask of composure against the torrent of emotion threatening to overwhelm her. She wouldn't cry. Not now. Not in front of Margaret.

"I'll think about it," she managed to say, her voice thin but firm.

Margaret nodded, her decision made, her duty discharged. "You've got a week, Elsie. To make up your mind. Then I make the arrangements, one way or another. For the farm. For you." With that, she turned and left, leaving Elsie standing alone in the doorway, the cold air seeping into the cottage, carrying with it the undeniable chill of an ultimatum.

A Final Letter, A Fierce Resolve
That night, the cottage felt colder, larger, imbued with a new, profound sense of isolation. Elsie lit a single candle on the mantle, its small flame flickering bravely, casting long, dancing shadows on the walls. She took out her notebook, its familiar pages a silent confidante.

She stared at the blank page for a long while, the empty space seeming to swallow her thoughts. Her hand, usually so steady when writing, trembled slightly. This was it. The final, unspoken truth. The one she had held closest, shielded most fiercely. Then, slowly, deliberately, her pen began to move, forming the familiar address.

"My Dearest Thomas," she wrote, her script perhaps a little tighter than usual, a reflection of the immense pressure she felt. "This may be the last letter I write you, my love. Not because I want to stop, not because my heart has forgotten you for a single moment, but because I must begin doing things, making choices, that leave no room for dreaming, for the indulgence of endless hope. The snow has come and gone twice since your last letter, a cruel passage of time. The orchard looks like bone now, stark and barren, mirroring the desolation I sometimes feel."

"I think of you still. Constantly. I think of the night you left, of the promise you made to return, and the promise I made to wait. I believe you meant it, Thomas. I believe you would be here if you could. Even if the war had other, more terrible plans. Even if fate has been cruel beyond imagining."

"I wish I could wait forever, Thomas. I wish I could simply suspend time, hold onto the last moments we shared. But I'm not waiting alone anymore. Not truly. He grows stronger every day within me. I feel him. A constant flutter, a gentle pressure, a profound, undeniable movement. A new heartbeat that echoes your own."

"I will raise him with kindness, Thomas. With every ounce of love I possess. With the stories of who you were, the man you stood for, the quiet strength and profound goodness I saw in you. If you return, he will know you. And if you don't... he will still know love. He will know of his father. He will know of our impossible, unwavering love. I will see to it."

"Yours always, Elsie"

She folded the letter carefully, meticulously, pressing its edges flat. She tied it with a fresh length of ribbon, a deep, vibrant red, a colour that spoke of life and defiant love, a stark contrast to the quiet despair in her heart. Then she walked across the cottage, her steps measured, her movements imbued with a new, solemn purpose. She knelt, lifted the loose floorboard, and placed the letter gently on top of the others, a new layer to the hidden history, a testament to a promise made in the face of impossible odds.

It was quieter now in the cottage, even than usual. The kind of quiet that settles not with peace or calm, but with the weighty finality of a momentous decision, an unalterable path. The air seemed to hum with unspoken consequences.

She rose, wrapping herself tightly in a blanket, its wool scratchy against her skin, and carried a cup of weak, now cold tea to the window. The orchard was still visible in the moonlight, its bare branches a hauntingly beautiful silhouette against the muted sky, the frost silvering the grass and the lower branches. She imagined Thomas walking through it again, his coat brushing the brittle leaves, his hands reaching for her, his eyes full of the promise of return, even as she carried the stark truth of his continued absence.

The cottage creaked around her, old and worn and full of silence. But it was a comforting kind of quiet now—the kind that made room for thoughts to stretch, for new, terrifying realities to solidify. It was no longer the silence of simple absence, but the quiet of profound change, of deep, quiet understanding, of an unalterable fate.

She thought of her parents. What would they say? The shame, the scandal, the absolute shattering of all expectations. She hadn't written to them in weeks, the distance between them growing not just in miles, but in the incomprehensible chasm of her secret. How could she begin to tell them about Thomas, a man who might be gone forever? About the child, a living consequence of a love they would never understand, could never accept?

She had considered leaving, taking a train somewhere, anywhere, and starting fresh in a city where no one knew her name, where her past could be shed like an old skin. But the orchard rooted her, its gnarled branches reaching deep into the earth, holding her fast. The letters, the hidden chronicle of her love, grounded her. The idea of him—of them—was not something she could leave behind. This was her home now. This was where she would wait. This was where she would begin.

Margaret had said they would manage. And for the first time, Elsie felt a flicker of belief in that gruff, compassionate promise. But she knew the weeks and months ahead would be long. Her body would change, visibly so. Whispers would inevitably start in the small, insular village. The war wouldn't wait for her to find her footing, wouldn't pause for her private revolution. The world would not be kind.

Still, she stayed by the window until her tea went cold, until the moonlight faded and the first faint streaks of dawn appeared on the horizon, painting the sky in a bruised palette of purples and greys. She watched the orchard, a silent sentinel of her love and her profound new reality. And somewhere in the vast, cold dark, into the indifferent expanse of the night, she whispered a promise to the wind, a fierce, unwavering vow not just for herself, but for the tiny, precious life within her, for the child she would soon bring into this chaotic world:

"I'll raise this child with love. Fierce, unwavering love. With every ounce of strength I possess. Even if I have to do it alone. Even if you never come back."

And somewhere in the vast, cold dark, the silence seemed to shift, as if the very air acknowledged her vow, absorbing it into the timeless fabric of the land, a solemn testament to a mother's unbreakable will.

# Chapter Sixteen

This chapter confirms Elsie's birth and the child's placement, drawing Sophie closer to the central revelation. I will expand it to over 3000 words by intensifying Sophie's physical and emotional exhaustion, detailing the atmosphere of the archive and the search process, and deepening her reflections on the converging truths of Elsie's secret and her father's unacknowledged past. The core plot points will remain unchanged.

Chapter 16: The Hidden Birth
The morning light, pale and diffuse, filtered into the cottage bathroom, reflecting off the mirror as Sophie stood before it, brushing steam from the glass with the side of her hand. The reflection that looked back at her was stark, unforgiving: a pale, drawn face, eyes shadowed with a profound, bone-deep tiredness she hadn't fully realized until this quiet, unflinching moment. It had been two weeks since her father's funeral, a blur of solemn rituals and hushed condolences. She still hadn't told her mum about the shocking discovery in the attic – the raw, desperate letter from Elsie, the tiny, fragile baby booties, Elsie's written confession. Somehow, the words hadn't found shape on her tongue, caught in a tangle of grief, apprehension, and an instinctual desire to protect her already-fragile mother. The secret felt too vast, too deeply rooted in a past that felt increasingly intertwined with her own present.

The cottage, with its quiet corners and hidden histories, had become her refuge once more, a silent sanctuary from the overwhelming reality of her loss and the daunting implications of Elsie's secret. Today, however, she was ready to pick up where she'd left off. The sealed envelope from

Elsie, now opened and reread a dozen times, its words imprinted on her thoughts, lay on the kitchen table, a constant, compelling presence. Its profound, heartbreaking confession had only deepened her resolve.

Ben was due to meet her in town later that morning. Their destination: the old council offices, a repository of local birth and adoption records – or what little remained from the chaotic war years, when official processes were often strained, incomplete, or simply overlooked. It was a daunting prospect, a dive into the administrative shadows of a bygone era.

The ride into town was quiet, the world outside hushed by a fresh blanket of snow. Thick drifts covered the verges, transforming the familiar landscape into a pristine, almost ethereal expanse of white, but melting into grey, treacherous slush along the well-travelled roads. The old car's tires hummed softly on the wet asphalt, a meditative sound that allowed Sophie's thoughts to drift, to settle. She parked just outside the unassuming, grey-stone building Ben had described, its façade blending into the muted winter sky. He was already waiting near the entrance, a familiar, reassuring silhouette, bundled in his usual navy coat, his notebook clutched in one gloved hand. A wisp of his breath plumed in the cold air.

"Hey," he said gently, his voice soft, his gaze immediately assessing her face. His usual slightly crooked smile was there, but it quickly faded as he took in the lingering exhaustion in her eyes, the drawn set of her mouth. "You okay, Sophie? You look... like you haven't been sleeping."

Sophie managed a small, tired nod. "As I'll ever be, I suppose. Come in." She stepped back, holding the heavy door open, allowing him to pass into the warmer interior. The air inside smelled faintly of old paper and the pervasive, almost sterile scent of disinfectant.

They stepped inside, shaking off the lingering cold. Ben removed his scarf, pushing his glasses up his nose, his movements economical. He followed her through a short corridor and into the main archive room. It smelled distinctly of old paper and cold stone, a scent both musty and strangely comforting. A volunteer archivist, a white-haired woman with a brisk, no-nonsense demeanour, greeted them with a nod and pointed them toward a section of records stored in aging, grey metal drawers that lined the wall. Ben explained their purpose, his voice low and professional — tracing a child born in Spring 1942, possibly at a mother-and-baby home, a delicate and often obscured area of wartime history. The volunteer gave them a knowing, sympathetic glance, and left them to their work.

"I can start by checking the parish birth registers from that period," Ben suggested, his voice quiet, already in work mode. "They were sometimes more detailed, or at least more consistent, than council records during the war. You can look through these council logs here — perhaps something about the Sisters of Mercy Home, if it operated in this area and kept records here. It's a long shot, but worth checking."

They split up, settling into the quiet rhythm of research. Sophie pulled out a rolling chair and began sifting through heavy, cumbersome files, many of them handwritten in fading, looping ink. Most of the documents she encountered were administrative—dry, mundane records of food requisitions for local businesses, property permits for new farm structures, occasional council meeting minutes. Each page was a faint echo of daily life, but yielded no direct answers to the profound questions burning in her mind. The air was thick with dust, rising in faint clouds with every opened folder, catching the light from the tall, narrow windows. She ran her fingers across the brittle paper, feeling the texture of decades, the weight of untold stories. But her attention was drawn, almost magnetically, to one thin, unassuming folder, its pale label, handwritten in a spidery script, catching her eye: PRIVATE PLACEMENTS – 1942.

She pulled it out, her heart quickening its pace, a sudden surge of adrenaline. She flipped it open, her movements precise, careful.

Only a few sheets remained within the folder, their fragility indicating their age and perhaps, their sensitive nature. One, yellowed and brittle, thinner than the others, contained a single, stark reference:

Miss E. Hale – temporary ward placement, Sisters of Mercy Home, Lincoln – March 1942

There was no child's name. No further details. No follow-up record of the infant. Just a terse, chilling note scrawled at the bottom in a different hand, a brief, impersonal summation: Case closed: child placed by order of parish intermediary. The words hung in the air, cold and official, confirming Elsie's confession. She had gone to a mother-and-baby home. She had given up her child.

Sophie copied the entry down, her hand trembling slightly, the pen scratching faintly on her notebook paper. She returned the folder to its place, her mind reeling, and walked slowly back to the main table where Ben was diligently sifting through a large, leather-bound register. He joined her moments later, a small slip of paper held carefully in his hand, a look of quiet triumph on his face.

"Found something, Sophie," he said, his voice low, a note of careful excitement. He held out the slip of paper. "It's a birth entry from a small parish church register, one that was notoriously meticulous. There's a record for April 1942—an unnamed male infant, mother listed as Elsie Hale. No father recorded, as expected, given the circumstances of the time."

Sophie stared at the words scrawled on the slip of paper. They blurred slightly, then sharpened into devastating clarity. Unnamed male. Mother: Elsie Hale. April 1942. It was him. The child. The direct, undeniable link. The son Elsie had given up.

"That's him," she said quietly, her voice barely a whisper, the confirmation settling over her with a profound, heavy finality. It was no longer just a suspicion, a pieced-together theory. It was fact.

Ben nodded, his expression sympathetic, confirming her unspoken thought. "It's a direct match, Elsie's presence at the home and the timing of the birth record. All points to the same truth."

"But there's no adoption record here?" Sophie asked, her mind already racing, searching for the next piece of the puzzle, for the fate of this unnamed boy.

"Not here, unfortunately," he replied, shaking his head. "That would have been handled through the church's own private records, or potentially a private solicitor if Elsie arranged it herself. Those records are much harder to access, usually sealed for decades, sometimes indefinitely. But this is a significant step forward. It means the child was formally registered, even if unnamed."

Sophie felt the full weight of it settle over her, a crushing burden of sorrow and understanding. A child. A boy. Born just months after Thomas's last heartbreaking letter, his final declaration of love. Born into a world without a father, then separated from his mother, raised somewhere else. No name given at birth, no public history she could see, only a numerical designation, a cold, official mark in an old book.

"Are you okay?" Ben asked gently, his hand reaching out instinctively, hovering above hers, offering a silent gesture of support.

She blinked, coming back to the present moment, her gaze finding his. "Yeah. I just... it's real now. All of it. The scale of her secret. The sacrifice." Her voice was thick with emotion, raw with unshed tears.

They sat in silence for a moment, the quiet of the archive a profound backdrop to their shared discovery. The fire crackled softly in a distant fireplace, a comforting sound. Then Ben broke the silence, his voice thoughtful. "There's someone I can call. An old colleague, a woman who used to volunteer extensively with the church archives across Lincolnshire. She has an encyclopaedic knowledge of these things, and crucially, access to some of those private records. If anyone has a chance of finding details about that adoption, it's her."

Sophie looked at him gratefully, a fresh wave of appreciation washing over her. "Thank you, Ben. Truly. For all of this. For listening. For helping."

He gave her a soft, genuine smile, a warm reassurance that spread to his eyes. "Don't thank me yet, Sophie. We're in it now. Together."

On the drive back to the cottage, the snow beginning to fall a little heavier, coating the windscreen in a fine, white film, Sophie didn't say much. She let the quiet sink in, letting the profound weight of her discoveries settle over her. Her mind returned again and again to the unnamed child in the record. No name. No public trace beyond a date and a mother's unacknowledged entry.

She thought of her father. Of his childhood photos—the ones that, she now realized with a sharp, painful jolt, always began when he was already three or four. No baby pictures. No clear, official birth certificate among the family records, something she had always just dismissed as an oversight, or a quirky family habit. She had always thought that was normal, or simply overlooked it, never questioning the blankness of his earliest years.

Now she wasn't so sure. The pieces were falling into place with a terrifying, undeniable logic. Elsie's hidden love. Thomas's disappearance. The secret birth. The child given up. Her father's missing early history. The implications were vast, dizzying.

Back at the cottage, she stood in the sitting room, the snow falling softly outside the window. In one hand, she held the fragile, pale blue baby booties. In the other, the stark, official copy of the birth record—Unnamed Male, Mother: Elsie Hale, April 1942.

Elsie, her great-aunt. The woman no one had ever spoken much about, shrouded in a veil of polite indifference. Who had lived alone in this quiet cottage. Who had died alone. Who had left behind a trail of breadcrumbs, of letters and hidden secrets, waiting for someone to find them, to piece together her unspoken truth.

Sophie sat down at the kitchen table, the silence of the cottage pressing in around her. She opened her journal, its blank pages a silent invitation, and began to write, her pen scratching across the paper with a new, urgent purpose.

He was real. He was born in April 1942. An unnamed male, born to Elsie Hale. No father listed. Born just months after Thomas's last letter, his final promise.

She gave him up. For his safety, for his future, for a chance at a normal life. She let him go into the world, without her. And now I think he might be someone I've known my whole life. Someone profoundly close.

She paused, her pen hovering over the page, her heart pounding a frantic rhythm. The next sentence, the logical conclusion, hovered at the edge of her thoughts, a terrifying, exhilarating truth.

She wasn't ready to write the next sentence. Not yet. Not until she had more proof. Not until she could speak it aloud without the overwhelming weight of tears. The name of the child, the man who was perhaps her own father, felt too sacred, too overwhelming to commit to paper without absolute certainty. The final piece of the puzzle, the last undeniable link, was still missing.

# Chapter Seventeen

The morning following her discovery of the baby booties and Elsie's heartbreaking confession in the attic, Sophie woke with a profound sense of purpose. The dull ache of grief for her father still lay heavy in her chest, a constant, underlying thrum, but now it was interwoven with a fierce, almost desperate urgency to uncover the truth. The pieces of Elsie's life, once scattered fragments, were beginning to coalesce into a terrifying, undeniable picture – a picture that now directly implicated her own family, her own father. The weight of that potential revelation was immense, pressing down on her even as it propelled her forward.

She made a hurried cup of tea, barely tasting it, and checked her phone. No reply from Ben yet, but it was still early. Her email, stark and brief, outlining the new discoveries, felt almost inadequate to convey the enormity of what she'd found. She paced the kitchen, unable to sit still, her gaze repeatedly drawn to the envelope with Elsie's final confession, and the tiny, impossibly fragile baby booties that lay beside it on the table. They were no longer just relics of the past; they were living, breathing evidence of a life unacknowledged, a secret fiercely guarded.

By mid-morning, Ben's reply finally pinged into her inbox. It was as brief as hers: On my way now. Give me half an hour. – Ben. The simple words brought an unexpected wave of relief. She wasn't alone in this. Not anymore.

When he arrived, the air outside still holding a sharp, wintry bite, he stepped into the cottage, his presence a solid, grounding force. He didn't ask questions immediately. He simply took in the scene on the kitchen table – the letter, the booties, the look of profound exhaustion and restless determination on Sophie's face. He poured himself a cup of the cooling tea Sophie had forgotten, and sat down, his gaze calm and steady.

"It's him, isn't it?" he said, his voice low, understanding. "Your father."

Sophie swallowed, her throat dry. She hadn't spoken the words aloud, not even to herself. Hearing them from Ben, uttered so simply, was a jolt. "I... I think so. It fits. The date of birth, the missing baby photos, my mum's silences about Elsie. It all... it all makes a terrible kind of sense." Her voice was hoarse, thick with unshed tears. "She named him in her head. And then she had to let him go. For his safety, she said. For his future."

Ben picked up one of the booties, turning it gently in his hand. "A brutal choice. But one made by many women during the war. Unmarried mothers, absent fathers... adoption was often seen as the only way for the child to have a chance at a 'normal' life." He paused, his gaze meeting hers. "If we're going to confirm this, we need to find the adoption records. It's a closed world, but my colleague, Eleanor, might be our best bet."

He spent the next hour on the phone, his voice a low, focused murmur from the sitting room. Sophie could hear snippets: "Private placements... Sisters of Mercy Home, Lincoln... early 1942... specific circumstances." She busied herself with tidying, a mindless activity that anchored her, but her ears strained, catching every fragment. Finally, he returned, a look of focused determination on his face.

"Eleanor is a miracle worker," he announced, running a hand through his hair. "She remembers the Sisters of Mercy Home in Lincoln. They were quite active during the war. She's found a faint trail, a handwritten entry in a subsidiary ledger, mentioning a placement by a 'parish intermediary' in April 1942. There's no name of the child or adoptive parents in that particular ledger, but she recalls another set of records, an older register, that might be more detailed. It's stored in a small, dusty annex of a church archive in a village called Market Rasen, about an hour from here. It's not usually open to the public, but Eleanor has a contact there, a retired vicar who's very protective of those records but trusts her implicitly. She's making a call for us."

Sophie felt a jolt of nervous energy. Market Rasen. Another small, anonymous village holding a potential key to her family's most profound secret. The hope, fragile but insistent, began to flutter in her chest.

They left soon after, the cottage settling into its familiar quiet behind them. The drive was tense, filled with unspoken anticipation. The Lincolnshire landscape, usually so flat and open, seemed to press in around them, the narrow country roads winding through fields still grey and stark under a low, heavy sky. Sophie's thoughts were a maelstrom. She pictured her father as a young boy, her mind frantically sifting through old family albums, trying to overlay the image of a spirited, mischievous child with the devastating knowledge that he might have been, for the first few years of his life, someone else entirely. Unnamed. Given away.

Ben drove calmly, his presence a steady anchor. He occasionally glanced at her, offering a quiet, comforting presence. He understood the immense emotional weight of this search. He understood that this wasn't just historical research; it was a deeply personal quest, a search for identity, for a missing piece of a beloved parent.

"This kind of record-keeping from that era was often... sparse," Ben explained, breaking the silence as they neared Market Rasen. "They prioritized privacy, and often, discretion over comprehensive documentation, especially in cases like this. Many birth names were changed, identities completely erased. It was done for protection, for the child's future, to prevent stigma. But it also means lives were hidden, histories lost."

Sophie nodded, her throat tight. "Elsie said she had to let him go for his safety. To give him something beautiful." Her voice was a raw whisper. "I wonder if he ever knew."

"We're about to find out," Ben said softly, pulling the car onto a quiet side street lined with terraced houses. The village of Market Rasen was larger than Fairfield, but still quaint, centered around a traditional market square. The church, an imposing stone structure with a tall spire, dominated the skyline. The annex Eleanor had described was a smaller, nondescript building tucked behind the main church, almost hidden by an ancient yew tree.

The Fateful Discovery
They were met by an elderly gentleman, Reverend Davies, a man with a shock of white hair and keen, surprisingly youthful eyes. He greeted Ben warmly, his trust in Eleanor evident. He led them through a narrow, echoing hallway that smelled of beeswax polish and damp stone, into a small, unheated room filled with heavy wooden shelves crammed

with old ledgers and dusty boxes. The air was thick with the scent of aged paper, a pervasive smell of history.

"Eleanor explained your sensitive inquiry," Reverend Davies said, his voice quiet, almost reverent, as he gestured to a large, leather-bound book open on a central table. "This is our Register of Private Baptisms and Placements. It was kept meticulously by Sister Agnes, one of the Sisters of Mercy. She was a remarkable woman. Very compassionate."

Sophie's heart began to thud, a frantic drumbeat against her ribs. This was it. The moment. She exchanged a glance with Ben, who gave her a small, encouraging nod.

Reverend Davies turned the brittle pages slowly, his finger tracing the faded ink. The pages were filled with names, dates, terse notes. Each entry represented a hidden life, a secret choice. He paused at a particular page, marked with a small, yellowed slip of paper.

"Here we are," he murmured, his voice soft. "An entry from April 1942. 'Infant Male. Mother's name: Elsie Hale.' And then a notation here, a placement record..." He leaned closer, squinting at the faded script. "...Placed with Mr. and Mrs. Arthur and Clara Mercer of Long Sutton. Adopted name: Edward Mercer. Baptism performed, June 1942."

The words, spoken so calmly, so matter-of-factly, hit Sophie with the force of a physical blow. Her vision swam. Edward Mercer. Her father's name. Her father's birth name. The truth, long suspected, now undeniable, concrete.

Sophie felt the blood drain from her face, leaving her cold and lightheaded. A profound gasp escaped her lips, a sound halfway between a sob and a choked cry. Her father. Her quiet, stoic father, had been Elsie's hidden child. He had been born in this world without a name, then given away, adopted by strangers, never knowing the extraordinary story of his birth, the profound love and sacrifice that had defined his beginning. The realization was a dizzying kaleidoscope of emotions: shock, sorrow, an overwhelming sense of Elsie's unimaginable pain, and a raw, aching grief for the father she thought she knew, who had carried this secret within him, unknowingly, his entire life.

Ben, ever observant, immediately put a hand on her arm, his touch firm and steady. "Sophie? Are you alright?" His voice was gentle, filled with concern.

She shook her head, tears finally, uncontrollably, blurring her vision, streaming down her face. This wasn't the quiet, contained grief she'd experienced at the funeral. This was raw, visceral, a torrent of emotion unleashed. "Edward Mercer," she whispered, the name catching in her throat, thick with tears. "My father. His name was Edward. He was Elsie's son." The words felt strange, alien, yet profoundly true as she spoke them aloud for the first time.

Reverend Davies, his face etched with understanding, looked at her with immense compassion. "So, he was your father, then?" he asked softly, his voice full of gentle sorrow. "I see. The thread continues."

Sophie could only nod, tears silently tracing paths down her cheeks. The threads. The breadcrumbs. They had led her directly to this impossible, heartbreaking truth. Her father, the man she knew, the man she had just buried, was the anonymous child, the boy Elsie had given up in the desperate hope of a better life. He had lived his entire life with this unspoken legacy woven into his very being, a profound secret he never knew to seek.

## A Reconfigured Past

She stared at the faded ink on the page: "Edward Mercer." The name of the man she knew as her father, etched into a record that revealed his true origins, his connection to a love story born of war and unimaginable sacrifice. It reconfigured everything. Her father's quiet nature, his occasional reticence about his early childhood, the lack of baby photos – all of it clicked into place with a devastating clarity. He wasn't just her father; he was the physical embodiment of Elsie and Thomas's hidden love, their impossible dream made real, then lost.

Ben squeezed her arm gently. "Take your time, Sophie. This is… a lot." He gave a quiet, respectful nod to Reverend Davies, who discreetly moved to a distant shelf, giving them space.

Sophie pressed her hand against her chest, as if to calm the frantic beating of her heart. The pain of her father's death, still so fresh, was now intertwined with a profound new layer of grief – grief for the child he had been, grief for the truth he never knew, grief for Elsie's unbearable sacrifice. She thought of her father's kind, sometimes gruff, eyes. Had there been a flicker of Elsie in them she had never seen? Had his stoicism been, in part, a legacy of the unacknowledged trauma of his early separation?

She looked at Ben, her eyes still wet but now filled with a fierce determination. "He never knew," she whispered, the words heavy with sorrow. "He lived his whole life… thinking his parents were Arthur and Clara Mercer. Never knowing his true mother. Never knowing Thomas Ashford, the man who loved her so fiercely."

Ben nodded, his expression solemn. "The secrecy of those times was absolute. It was meant to protect, but it often meant lives were built on foundations of unspoken truths. He would have been too young to remember Elsie or his early days at the home."

"But Elsie remembered him," Sophie insisted, clutching the printout of the adoption record as if it might disappear. "She remembered him every day. She kept his booties. She wrote that letter for him, for 'when the time is right.' She carried this secret alone for decades." The enormity of Elsie's burden, her lifelong quiet suffering, was almost unbearable to contemplate.

Ben reached for his notebook, his movements quiet, efficient. "We have the full name now, Edward Mercer. That's a game-changer. We can cross-reference with census records, military service records for him. We can start to build a clearer picture of his adoptive family, his life. And perhaps, even find out if Arthur and Clara Mercer had other children, other family members who might still be alive." He paused, his gaze gentle. "It's a huge revelation, Sophie. But it also means you're closer to understanding everything. To piecing together the complete story."

Sophie nodded, slowly, absorbing his words. The overwhelming rush of emotion was beginning to recede, leaving behind a clear, sharp sense of purpose. The mystery wasn't just about Elsie and Thomas anymore; it was about her father, about her own lineage, about the very roots of who she was.

"Thank you, Ben," she said, her voice stronger now, though still thick with the residue of tears. "Thank you for finding this. For being here."

He smiled, a gentle, understanding expression. "We're in it, remember? And this is what I do. It's a privilege to help uncover such an important piece of history." He hesitated, then added, his voice lower, "And Sophie... you're not alone. Not with this. Not with your grief."

She met his gaze, a quiet gratitude passing between them. His steady presence, his unwavering support, was a profound comfort in the face of such overwhelming truths. She knew then that this journey, though born of sorrow and ancient secrets, was also bringing something new into her life, something unexpected and quietly vital.

As they walked out of the quiet archive, the cold air bracing, Sophie felt a shift within her. The weight of the world, though still heavy with loss, was no longer entirely on her shoulders. She had found a profound truth, and she had found an unexpected ally. The path ahead was still uncertain, still filled with questions, but for the first time in a very long time, she felt a quiet strength, a renewed sense of purpose. The story was not just Elsie's, or Thomas's, or even her father's anymore. It was Sophie's to tell. And she was ready.

# Chapter Eighteen

The drive back to the cottage from Market Rasen was a blur of muted landscape and swirling thoughts for Sophie. The revelation of her father's true identity, the stark, undeniable name on the adoption record—Edward Mercer, born to Elsie Hale—felt like a seismic shift in the very foundations of her world. The snow, falling gently, seemed to muffle the sounds outside, amplifying the thunderous silence within the car, within her own mind. Ben drove with a quiet, respectful focus, occasionally glancing her way, his presence a steady, anchoring force in the tempest of her emotions. She barely registered the journey, her gaze fixed on the endless grey ribbon of road, yet seeing nothing but the unfolding panorama of Elsie's sacrifice and her father's unacknowledged past.

When they finally arrived back at the cottage, the familiar stone walls offered a sense of fragile comfort, a silent witness to the history she was so desperately trying to unearth. She stepped inside, the cold air bracing, and dropped her bag by the door, the small thud echoing in the quiet. Ben followed, his face etched with concern. He didn't press her, didn't try to force conversation. He simply placed a comforting hand on her shoulder before moving towards the fireplace, instinctively beginning to build a fire, the rhythmic sound of kindling catching a welcome distraction.

Sophie found herself drawn to the old, leather-bound photo album she had found days ago but had been unable to open. Now, with the truth throbbing in her veins, she picked it up, her fingers tracing the worn binding. She carried it to the kitchen table, where Elsie's final letter still lay open, beside the tiny baby booties. The juxtaposition was stark: the raw, personal confession of Elsie's love and loss, and the silent, captured images of the man who was Elsie's son, Edward. Her father.

She opened the album, her hands trembling. Page after page of sepia and faded colour photographs. Her father as a boy, a mischievous grin on his face, a missing front tooth. Her father as a young man, gangly and awkward at family holidays. Her father, stern yet kind, holding her hand as a child. She looked at each image with new eyes, searching for a trace of Elsie, a ghost of Thomas, a hint of the truth that had been hidden beneath the surface of his life. Did the stoic set of his jaw come from Elsie's quiet strength? Did the occasional faraway look in his eyes betray an unconscious yearning for a past he never knew? The grief for him, still a heavy stone in her chest, was now compounded by a profound, aching sorrow for the secret he carried, unknowingly, to his grave.

She wanted to call her mother. The urge was a physical ache, a desperate need to share this monumental discovery, to unburden herself of the truth. But how? How could she shatter her mother's carefully constructed world, her memories of a stable, predictable marriage, with such an astonishing revelation? Her mother was still grieving, fragile, barely able to process the sudden void her father's death had left. To tell her now felt cruel, a double blow that might break her completely. So, the words remained unsaid, trapped behind her lips, adding another layer of complex silence to the cottage. She would wait. She had to.

Ben's Quiet Pursuit

As Sophie sat, lost in the labyrinth of her family's past, Ben worked quietly in the background. He recognized the profound need for space Sophie had in that moment, understanding that such a revelation demanded solitary processing. He stoked the fire until it blazed cheerfully, pushing back the damp chill of the cottage, filling the air with the comforting scent of woodsmoke. He boiled the kettle, made fresh tea, and placed a mug silently by Sophie's hand, a wordless gesture of support. Then, he retreated to the small study, already picking up his phone, his mind shifting gears back to the methodical pursuit of information.

His research began immediately. He started by calling Eleanor Vance, the retired archivist who had provided the initial lead. Her quiet patience and vast, almost encyclopaedic knowledge of Lincolnshire's hidden histories were invaluable. He explained the confirmed connection to Edward Mercer, Sophie's father, and the new objective: to trace Edward's life after his adoption. This meant delving into the records of Arthur and Clara Mercer, his adoptive parents in Long Sutton.

"The Mercers," Eleanor mused over the phone, her voice a faint crackle but clear. "Ah, yes. A respectable family, I believe. Market gardeners, mostly. Smallholding. Always kept to themselves. I recall Arthur was a pillar of the local chapel, quite devout." She promised to check local census records, old land registry documents, and any church records pertaining to the Mercer family in Long Sutton from 1942 onwards. "It'll take a bit of digging, Ben. You know how these things are. People often moved, names changed. But if Edward was indeed their adopted son, there will be traces."

Ben also cast a wider net, reaching out to contacts in adoption history societies, knowing that private adoptions in the 1940s often left faint, hard-to-follow trails. He cross-referenced names, dates, and locations, meticulously building a profile of the Mercer family.

Over the next two days, the cottage became a silent hub of historical investigation. Sophie moved between moments of profound grief and intense focus. She spent hours poring over the letters again, now reading them with the full, devastating knowledge of Elsie's pregnancy and ultimate sacrifice. Elsie's anxieties, her desperate hope for Thomas's return to know his child, resonated with a new, sharper ache. Sophie saw Elsie not just as a historical figure, but as a young woman caught in an impossible bind, a mother whose love was so fierce she chose anonymity for her child's perceived welfare.

Ben, meanwhile, meticulously pieced together the fragments of the Mercer family history. He found census records from 1951 listing Arthur and Clara Mercer in Long Sutton, and indeed, a young Edward, aged nine. There was no mention of any other children, suggesting Edward was either an only child or his siblings were significantly older and had already left home. He found records of Arthur Mercer's small market garden, and Clara's involvement in the local Women's Institute. It was a picture of quiet, respectable rural life, seemingly devoid of secrets.

"It's a solid paper trail for Edward from 1942 onwards," Ben explained one evening, sitting at the kitchen table with Sophie, a stack of printouts between them. "He attended the local school, then left at 15, common for the time, likely to work on the farm. He registered for national service in the late 1950s, but was deemed unfit for active duty due to a childhood leg injury – a detail that piqued my interest.

Perhaps a legacy of his early life, before the Mercers?" He looked at Sophie, a question in his eyes.

Sophie's mind immediately flashed to Thomas's own leg injury, his shrapnel wound from Dunkirk. Was it possible that the "childhood leg injury" was a genetic predisposition, or perhaps even a subtle birth defect inherited from Thomas? It was a tenuous link, but it added another layer to the confirmation. "My dad had a slight limp," Sophie confirmed, her voice quiet. "From an old sports injury, he always said. But it was always there, even when he was a boy."

Ben nodded, making a note. "Interesting. It adds weight. The records show Edward remained in Long Sutton until his early twenties, then moved away, eventually settling closer to Lincoln where he later met your mother, I presume."

"Yes," Sophie said, lost in thought. Her father had rarely spoken about his childhood, dismissing it as "boring farm stuff." She had always accepted that at face value. Now, she understood the unspoken reasons behind his reticence. Was it simply that he found it uninteresting, or was there a deeper, subconscious disconnect, a sense of not fully belonging, a feeling he couldn't articulate because he didn't know the truth?

A Journey to Long Sutton
The next morning, driven by a compelling need to connect with this newly discovered past, Sophie decided to visit Long Sutton. Ben offered to accompany her, his offer gentle but firm, and she accepted gratefully. She knew she couldn't face this particular ghost alone.

The drive was short, less than an hour from the cottage. Long Sutton was a larger, more bustling market town than Fairfield, but still retained a distinct rural charm. Old brick buildings lined the narrow high street, and the scent of freshly baked bread mingled with the damp earth. They walked past the busy shops, the familiar sounds of everyday life a stark contrast to the historical weight Sophie carried.

They found the street where the Mercers had lived using an old map Ben had printed. It was a quiet residential lane, lined with modest, semi-detached houses, their small gardens neat even in winter. The Mercer family home, Ben pointed out, was now painted a cheerful pale yellow, its front door adorned with a festive wreath, clearly inhabited by a different family. It felt surreal, standing on the very pavement where her father had played as a boy, where he had grown up, completely unaware of his true beginnings.

Sophie stood for a long time, simply staring at the house, trying to conjure an image of her father as a young boy inside those walls, being raised by people who were not his biological parents. It wasn't a sudden, shattering revelation, but a quiet, almost melancholic acceptance. The fact that the house was now occupied by strangers, their lives unfolding obliviously within its walls, felt strangely poignant. The secrets of the past were just that – secrets, contained and silent, while life moved on, oblivious.

They walked to the local cemetery, a peaceful expanse of weathered headstones and ancient yew trees. Ben, using his detailed research, quickly located the grave of Arthur and Clara Mercer. Their headstone was simple, unassuming, listing their birth and death dates. Arthur (1900-1975), Clara (1902-1980). They had lived long, quiet lives. Sophie stood there, looking at the names of the people who had raised her father, feeling a complex mix of gratitude and sorrow. They had given him a home, a life, a name. But they had also, presumably, kept the most fundamental truth from him.

"Eleanor also found a mention of Arthur and Clara being involved with the local Baptist Chapel," Ben explained, his voice low, respectful of the solemnity of the place. "They were apparently very active, particularly with outreach programs for displaced children during and after the war."

Sophie's head snapped up. "Displaced children?"

Ben nodded. "Yes. Many local churches had informal networks for placing children who were orphaned, evacuated, or, in some cases, born to single mothers during the war. It was often a very discreet process, handled within the church community, which would explain the lack of formal adoption records in the public archive. The 'parish intermediary' Elsie's record mentioned would likely have been a vicar or a church elder."

This added another layer of understanding to Elsie's agonizing choice. It wasn't a cold, impersonal system, but perhaps a network of concerned individuals, trying to do their best in impossible circumstances. And her father, Edward, had been placed with a family known for their compassion. It eased a small part of the profound sadness Sophie felt for Elsie.

A Glimmer of Connection
As they were leaving the cemetery, Ben's phone buzzed. He listened, then nodded, a look of triumph dawning on his face. "Eleanor. She's found a likely candidate. Arthur and Clara

Mercer had a niece, a distant cousin of Edward's through the Mercer side, who was born around the same time as him. She's still alive, in her late 80s now, and lives in a residential home not far from here. Her name is Mary Davies. Eleanor says she was quite close to her Aunt Clara."

Sophie's breath hitched. A living relative. Someone who might have known her father as a child, someone who might have observed the subtle dynamics of his adoption, or even heard whispers. This was more than records; this was memory.

"Can we... can we go see her?" Sophie asked, her voice thick with a mixture of apprehension and desperate hope.

"Eleanor's already called the home, explained the situation carefully, without revealing too much detail. Mary is a little frail, but lucid, and she's agreed to see us this afternoon. Says she always liked a good story." Ben's gaze met Sophie's, a quiet understanding passing between them. "This could be it, Sophie. The closest we'll get to a living witness."

The journey to the residential home was short, the anticipation building with every turn of the wheel. Sophie found herself instinctively reaching for the worn silver locket she now wore around her neck – Thomas's locket, which she had found tucked away in Elsie's journal, its clasp loose, its tiny picture of Elsie now her most cherished possession. She held it tight, a silent prayer to Elsie and Thomas, for courage, for clarity.

Ben, sensing her nerves, gently squeezed her arm. "Whatever we find, Sophie, remember Elsie's strength. And your father's. You carry both within you." His words were quiet, a simple reassurance, but they resonated deeply within her, a comforting warmth spreading through her veins. Their shared purpose, born from a historical mystery, had slowly, organically, evolved into a profound personal connection, a quiet understanding that transcended mere professional collaboration. In the face of overwhelming loss and shocking revelations, Ben had become her steadfast anchor, guiding her through the emotional labyrinth of her newfound past. His presence was more than professional; it was a quiet, unwavering comfort, a silent promise of support as she stood on the precipice of a truth that would reconfigure everything. The silence between them in the car was no longer empty, but filled with shared anticipation, a quiet understanding that they were navigating not just history, but a family's complex, hidden heart.

# Chapter Nineteen

The drive to the residential home where Mary Davies resided was surprisingly short from Market Rasen, cutting through the vast, open expanses of Lincolnshire that still lay under a pale, winter sky. Snow, a soft, ethereal white, had begun to fall again, dusting the already muted landscape, coating the bare hedgerows and the skeletal branches of distant trees. Inside the car, the quiet was profound, a weighty silence filled only by the soft hum of the engine and the rhythmic sweep of the wipers. Sophie felt a strange sense of unreality, as if she were moving through a dreamscape, heading towards a confrontation with a past that was simultaneously ancient and acutely present.

Her hands, resting lightly on her lap, were cold despite the car's heating, a fine tremor running through them. She instinctively reached for the small, worn silver locket that now hung around her neck, its cool metal a tangible link to Elsie and Thomas. Her thumb traced the faint inscription on its surface, a silent prayer. The thought of meeting someone who had known her father as a child, someone who had lived in the orbit of his adopted family, filled her with a nervous anticipation that almost eclipsed her lingering grief. This wasn't a dry archive record; this was living memory, a chance to hear a story, perhaps even a whisper of a truth, from someone who had witnessed it.

Ben, sensing her escalating tension, reached across the console and gently squeezed her arm. His touch was firm, grounding, a quiet reassurance that resonated deep within her. "You okay, Sophie?" he murmured, his gaze warm and steady. "It's a lot to take in. Remember what we talked about.

This is just about finding the truth. Whatever that truth may be."

She nodded, managing a small, watery smile. "I'm trying. It's just... it feels monumental. Like every piece of my life is being reassembled." She looked out at the falling snow, her breath pluming faintly against the cold glass. "My dad. All those unspoken things. It's like discovering he had a whole hidden life before he was even him."

Ben pulled into the neat, paved driveway of the residential home. It was a modern, red-brick building, welcoming and unassuming, with carefully manicured flowerbeds now blanketed in snow. The air smelled crisp, clean, and faintly of institutional polish. They were ushered into a bright, airy sitting room, filled with soft armchairs and the quiet murmur of other residents.

Mary Davies was seated in a winged armchair by a large window, a knitted shawl draped over her shoulders. She was small and frail, her movements slow, but her eyes, a faded blue, were remarkably sharp and alert, taking them in with a keen, assessing gaze. Her white hair was neatly pinned, and a faint, sweet scent of lavender clung to her. She looked precisely as a woman in her late eighties should – aged, but imbued with a quiet dignity and the deep wisdom of years.

"Mr. Taylor," she greeted Ben, her voice surprisingly clear, though a little reedy. "And you must be Elsie's... relation." Her gaze moved to Sophie, a flicker of something unreadable in her eyes.

"Yes, Mrs. Davies," Sophie said, stepping forward, feeling a sudden shyness. "I'm Sophie Mercer. Elsie Hale was my great-aunt. And... I believe your Aunt Clara and Uncle Arthur adopted her son, Edward."

Mary's lips parted in a small, surprised O. Her gaze sharpened, fixed intently on Sophie's face. She paused, then slowly, deliberately, she patted the arm of a nearby chair. "Sit, dear. Sit. And tell me. I remember Edward. Such a good boy. Always quiet."

They sat, and for the next hour, Mary Davies began to weave a tapestry of memory, her voice flowing, sometimes hesitant, sometimes remarkably lucid. She spoke of Arthur and Clara Mercer, describing them as devout, kindly people, pillar of their local Baptist Chapel, who longed for children but couldn't have their own. "They tried for years, you see. And then, the war. So many children orphaned, displaced. Clara, bless her heart, she said it was God's will. To give a home to one of God's lost little lambs."

Sophie listened, her heart aching. Elsie's secret, her desperate sacrifice, was now framed within the context of Clara and Arthur's longing.

"Edward arrived in the spring of '42," Mary continued, her eyes distant, lost in the past. "A tiny thing he was. Quiet. Never cried much. Clara adored him. Arthur, too. He was their miracle. They never spoke of his... origins. Not to us. Not directly. It was unspoken, you see. Like many things back then. A kindness, they thought. To give him a clean slate."

"Did Edward ever know he was adopted?" Sophie asked, her voice barely a whisper, the crucial question hanging in the air.

Mary paused, her gaze settling on Sophie, a deep sadness in her eyes. "He never did. Not from them, anyway. Clara and Arthur, they believed it best. To protect him. From the stigma, you understand. A child born out of wedlock, to a Land Girl... well, it wasn't spoken of. Not kindly, often. And his real father... well, Thomas Ashford, he was the talk of the village, too. Quiet, handsome. But a soldier from away. And then... missing. A tragedy." She shook her head, a sigh escaping her lips. "They wanted Edward to have a simple, good life. A proper name. A proper family."

Sophie felt tears prick at her eyes, a sharp ache in her chest. Her father. He had lived his entire life with this fundamental truth about himself concealed, a silent, unacknowledged orphan of war and impossible love. It was a profound, bittersweet tragedy.

"He was a good boy, Edward," Mary continued, oblivious to Sophie's quiet turmoil. "Always helping Arthur in the garden. Never complained. Kept to himself, though. Like Elsie. Funny that, isn't it? He had her quietness about him. I always noticed that. Different from Arthur's bluster or Clara's busy chatter. He had a way of just... watching. Observing."

Sophie remembered her father's own quiet nature, his contemplative silences. It wasn't just a personality trait, she realized now; it was a legacy, a resonance of his biological mother. The thought brought a fresh wave of tears.

Echoes of Resemblance
Mary went on, painting a vivid picture of Edward's childhood. His love for reading, for spending hours in the

quiet corners of the chapel library. His surprising talent for intricate woodwork, a steady hand and a meticulous eye. Elsie had worked on a farm, collected eggs, fixed fences. Thomas was "good with his hands." Sophie's father, Edward, had built intricate model ships in his garage workshop in retirement, a quiet, precise hobby that had consumed him for hours. The connections, once tenuous, now felt undeniably strong.

"He was always very close to Aunt Clara," Mary recalled, her voice softening. "She spoilt him rotten, some might say. She felt such... such gratitude, you see. For having him. As if he was a gift from heaven. And Arthur, well, Arthur was devoted. He taught Edward everything about the market garden, about the soil, about hard work. But Edward... he was always a bit of a dreamer, too. Didn't always have his head in the soil like Arthur. More interested in maps, and stories, and the world beyond Long Sutton."

Sophie listened intently, absorbing every detail. Her father, a dreamer? She had always known him as practical, grounded. But she remembered the old, oversized atlas he kept in his study, filled with annotations and circled places he'd never visited. His quiet fascination with historical documentaries. His love for old adventure novels. These details, once dismissed as mere hobbies, now took on a new, profound significance. They were glimpses of the hidden man, the boy who carried the unspoken legacy of a mother who loved stories and a father who had seen the world in the crucible of war.

"Did he ever seem curious about his birth, Mrs. Davies?" Sophie finally managed to ask, her voice barely audible. "Did he ever ask questions about Elsie, or about why he was with Arthur and Clara?"

Mary frowned, her brow furrowed in thought. "Not directly, dear. Never directly. Clara would have had a fit, bless her. But I remember one time, he was a teenager, a difficult age, and he found an old photograph. It was a picture of Clara and Arthur with some of the Land Girls, taken at some harvest festival. And Elsie was in it. He just... stared at it. For a long time. Didn't say anything. Just looked. And then he put it back. Never mentioned it again. But I saw him looking at Elsie. I always wondered." She looked at Sophie, a knowing glint in her pale eyes. "There was a resemblance, you see. Always was. Elsie, in her youth, she had that same quiet intensity you have, dear. And Edward... he had her eyes, I always thought. Those dark, serious eyes."

Sophie felt a jolt. Elsie's eyes. Her father's eyes. Her own eyes. The physical confirmation, spoken so casually by Mary, was profoundly unsettling, yet strangely comforting. The threads of connection, once invisible, were now brilliantly illuminated.

The conversation continued for a while longer, Mary sharing anecdotes, small glimpses into Edward's childhood, his quiet strengths, his particularities. She mentioned his devotion to his adoptive parents, his unwavering sense of duty, his eventual move away from Long Sutton for work. She confirmed that Arthur and Clara had indeed died peacefully in the late 1970s and early 1980s, respectively, never having revealed the truth to their beloved son.

As the interview drew to a close, Sophie felt a complex mix of emotions. A deep sorrow for her father, who had lived his life fundamentally unaware of his own origins. A profound respect and empathy for Elsie, who had carried such an immense burden of love and sacrifice. And a strange, quiet sense of peace. The questions that had gnawed at her, the blanks in her family history, were finally beginning to be filled.

The Weight of Truth, The Spark of Purpose
They thanked Mary Davies profusely, her quiet recollections a priceless gift. As they walked out of the residential home and back into the crisp, snowy afternoon, Sophie felt lighter, yet profoundly weighed down all at once. The air still carried the scent of wet snow and winter, but her perception of the world had irrevocably shifted.

"Well," Ben said quietly, breaking the silence as they reached his car. "That confirms it, doesn't it? Every piece. Elsie's son, Edward Mercer, your father. Adopted by Arthur and Clara. Never knew." His voice was gentle, recognizing the profound impact of the revelations.

Sophie nodded, unable to speak, tears stinging her eyes again, not of despair, but of overwhelming understanding. "All this time," she whispered, her voice raw. "He never knew. And Elsie... she lived her whole life, knowing. Waiting."

Ben put a hand on her shoulder, his fingers warm even through her coat. "She left the breadcrumbs for a reason, Sophie. For you to find. For her story to finally be told. For his, too."

They drove back to the cottage in companionable silence, the snow now falling more heavily, beginning to blanket the roads. Sophie's mind raced, processing the incredible narrative that had unfolded. Her father, the quiet, stoic man who had shaped her own childhood, was the direct, living link between Elsie's desperate wartime love and Sophie's present-day search for identity. The themes of lost love, emotional inheritance, and generational silence, which had seemed abstract before, were now profoundly personal, etched into the very fabric of her being.

Back in the cottage, the fire Ben had built earlier still offered a comforting warmth. Sophie sat at the kitchen table, the baby booties, Elsie's letter, Thomas's last letter, and now Ben's meticulous notes from Mary Davies spread out before her. The truth was laid bare, clear and undeniable.

She thought of her own journal, the one she had started writing in again. Elsie had said she had to "finish the story, whether anyone ever read it or not." But Elsie hadn't finished it. She had only started it, leaving the final chapters for someone else. For Sophie.

A quiet, yet powerful, resolve began to settle over Sophie. This story, this extraordinary, heartbreaking, beautiful story, could not remain buried. It deserved to be told, to be honoured, to finally breathe in the light. Not just for Elsie, or for Thomas, or for her father Edward, but for herself. To make sense of her own grief, her own past, her own place in this reconfigured family tree.

She looked at Ben, who was quietly brewing fresh tea, his silhouette solid and reassuring against the flickering firelight. He had been a steadfast presence through this storm of discovery, his quiet intelligence and unwavering empathy a constant anchor. He hadn't just helped her find the facts; he had helped her navigate the emotional landscape of the past.

"Ben," she said, her voice clear, resolute. "I've decided. I'm going to write a book. About Elsie. About Thomas. About... all of this."

He turned, a warm, gentle smile spreading across his face, his eyes crinkling at the corners. He understood. "That's a wonderful idea, Sophie. A powerful one." He walked over to the table and picked up Elsie's final letter, the one addressed "For when the time is right." "It's the least their story deserves."

He sat opposite her, the glow of the fire reflecting in his glasses. "And I'd be honoured to help you, if you'll let me. With the research. The context. Anything you need." His voice was low, and his gaze, as it met hers, held more than just professional dedication. It held a quiet understanding, a shared purpose that transcended the historical quest.

Sophie felt a warmth spread through her, a comforting sensation that went deeper than the fire's heat. It wasn't just about the book; it was about the path opening before her. The cottage creaked around them, old and full of secrets, but now, it also felt full of possibility. The snow continued to fall softly outside, blanketing the world in a pristine quiet, a fresh start. And in that shared silence, Sophie felt a profound sense of grounding, a connection to the past that surprisingly, irrevocably, pointed her towards a hopeful future. The ghosts weren't laid to rest yet, but they were finally ready to speak, and Sophie was ready to listen, and to write.

# Chapter Twenty

The days following the meeting with Mary Davies were a
blur of intense emotion and meticulous research for Sophie.
The confirmation that her quiet, grounded father, Edward
Mercer, was Elsie Hale's son, given up as an infant in the
desperate chaos of wartime 1942, sat in her chest like a heavy,
beating truth. It reconfigured everything: her childhood
memories, her understanding of her parents' marriage, the
very foundation of her identity. She found herself constantly
looking at old photographs of her father with new eyes,
searching for faint echoes of Elsie's solemn gaze, or
Thomas's quiet intensity, traces she now saw everywhere.

Grief for her father, still a raw wound, had morphed into
something more complex—a profound sorrow not just for his
absence, but for the fundamental truth about himself that he
had carried unknowingly to his grave. She imagined him as
that unnamed infant, a tiny bundle passed from one set of
loving hands to another, unaware of the immense sacrifice
that had led to his very existence. The weight of Elsie's
lifelong secret, her silent endurance, settled over Sophie like
a cloak.

The most daunting task loomed before her: telling her
mother. The thought was a constant knot in her stomach, a
profound anxiety that superseded all others. How could she,
Sophie, be the one to shatter her mother's reality, to unravel
the carefully constructed narrative of their family? Her
mother, already reeling from the sudden, brutal loss of her
husband, was fragile, barely navigating the new landscape of
widowhood. To add this astonishing, potentially painful
revelation felt almost cruel. Sophie rehearsed the words in
her head, over and over, discarding them, reshaping them,

trying to find a way to convey such a monumental truth with both tenderness and clarity.

She spoke to Ben about it, one evening, after another long day spent poring over digital archives in the cottage. The fire was low, casting flickering shadows on the walls, and the wind outside rattled the shutters like an impatient ghost.

"I don't know how to tell her, Ben," Sophie confessed, her voice thin, raw with fear. "How do you tell someone that the life they believed in, the man they loved for decades, had a beginning that was a complete secret? That he was given away? That his mother, my great-aunt, was really his birth mother?" She wrapped her arms around herself, as if physically bracing for the inevitable conversation.

Ben sat opposite her, his gaze steady, empathetic. He didn't offer platitudes, just quiet understanding. "There's no easy way, Sophie. No perfect words. It's a truth that will reshape everything for her. But perhaps... perhaps it's also a truth that can bring its own kind of healing. Your mother loved your father deeply. And the truth of his birth doesn't diminish that love, or his life with her. It just makes it... fuller. More complex. More poignant." He paused, his hand reaching across the table to cover hers, a gentle, comforting pressure. "You're not doing this to hurt her, Sophie. You're doing it because it's Elsie's truth. And your father's. And it's part of your story too, now. It deserves to be known."

His touch was grounding, his words a lifeline. Sophie squeezed his hand, grateful for his quiet strength, his unwavering belief in the importance of truth, even painful truth. In these intense weeks, Ben had become more than just a researcher; he was her confidante, her anchor, a silent witness to the profound reordering of her world. The connection between them had deepened into something undeniable, a shared understanding forged in the crucible of discovery.

The next morning, armed with Ben's quiet support and a desperate resolve, Sophie packed a small bag and drove towards her mother's house. The journey felt longer than usual, each mile a step closer to an emotional reckoning. The familiar landscape of Lincolnshire, usually a source of quiet comfort, now seemed to mirror her internal turmoil: grey, expectant, filled with an unspoken tension.

The Revelation
Her mother's house stood quietly on its suburban street, a familiar bastion of normality. Sophie hesitated at the front door, her hand hovering over the bell, her heart thudding. This was it. No turning back. She took a deep, fortifying breath and rang the doorbell.

Her mother answered, her face still etched with the raw grief of widowhood, but she managed a weak smile. "Sophie, darling. Come in. I wasn't expecting you today." Her eyes, though still red-rimmed, held a flicker of surprise, a momentary reprieve from her sorrow.

Sophie stepped inside, the familiar scent of her childhood home – her mother's perfume, polish, the faint aroma of cooked meals – now felt subtly altered, imbued with a new, strange atmosphere of impending revelation. She followed her mother into the sitting room, its tidy, comfortable décor a stark contrast to the tumultuous secret she carried.

"Mum," Sophie began, her voice a little shaky, but firm. She decided against preamble, against easing into it. The truth, blunt and direct, felt like the only way. "I need to tell you something. Something very important. It's about Dad. And about Elsie."

Her mother's brow furrowed, a flicker of apprehension in her eyes. "Elsie? What about Elsie, darling? And your father? What's happened?" Her voice held a note of rising alarm.

Sophie sat on the edge of the sofa, facing her mother, and took a deep breath. She started at the beginning, or rather, where her journey had begun. "When I went to the cottage, after Elsie's funeral… I found some letters. Hidden. Hundreds of them. From Elsie. To a soldier named Thomas Ashford." She spoke slowly, calmly, trying to control the tremble in her voice, watching her mother's face for every shift of emotion.

Her mother listened, her expression a mix of bewilderment and growing concern. "Letters? To a soldier? Elsie?" She shook her head, as if trying to clear it. "Elsie was always so private. Your father said she was a recluse even when he was a boy."

"Yes," Sophie confirmed. "But these letters… they were different. They were full of love. A fierce, powerful love. He was a soldier, Thomas Ashford. He was injured at Dunkirk, came to Ravenswick Farm to recover, where Elsie was a Land Girl. They fell in love. And then he was sent back to France, to Caen. His last letter arrived in November 1941. He went missing in early 1942. Never returned." Sophie kept her gaze steady, watching her mother's face as the story unfolded, layer by painful layer.

Her mother's eyes widened, a dawning comprehension slowly replacing the bewilderment. "Missing? A soldier? Elsie... my word." Her hand went to her mouth, a small, incredulous sound escaping her lips.

"And then," Sophie continued, her voice softer, bracing herself for the ultimate revelation, "in Elsie's attic, I found another hidden place. Behind a panel. And there... I found a letter from Elsie. Her last, profound confession. And with it... these." Sophie reached into her bag and pulled out the carefully wrapped baby booties, laying them gently on the coffee table between them. She then placed the scanned copy of the hospital record and the adoption record next to them.

Her mother stared at the tiny, faded blue booties, her breath catching. Her gaze then moved to the official-looking papers, her eyes scanning the words on the adoption certificate. Edward Mercer. Mother: Elsie Hale. April 1942. The names, so stark and undeniable, seemed to leap from the page.

Her mother's face went utterly, terrifyingly blank. The colour drained from her cheeks, leaving her ashen. She looked at the booties, then the documents, then at Sophie, her eyes wide, unfocused, searching. "No," she whispered, a ragged, guttural sound, filled with disbelief and pain. "No. That's... that's impossible. Edward was... Edward was Arthur and Clara's son. He was my husband. This... this can't be right."

Sophie reached for her mother's hand, clasping it firmly. "Mum, I know this is shocking. It was for me too. But the records are clear. I've spoken to a woman, Mary Davies, a distant relative of Arthur and Clara Mercer. She remembers Edward as a baby, remembers his arrival. She confirmed that

Arthur and Clara adopted him from the Sisters of Mercy Home in Lincoln. Elsie was his birth mother. And Thomas Ashford... he was his father."

Her mother pulled her hand away, her body recoiling, a visible tremor running through her. She leaned back against the sofa cushions, her eyes fixed on the distant wall, as if trying to escape the unbearable truth. Tears welled, not the gentle flow of grief, but harsh, racking sobs that shook her thin frame. "My Edward," she choked out, the name a broken whisper. "My husband. He never... he never knew. He never spoke of this. Not a word."

Sophie moved closer, putting an arm around her mother's trembling shoulders. "That's what Elsie's letter says, Mum. She said she had to give him up for his safety, for his future, for a normal life, because Thomas was gone and she was alone. She didn't want the stigma for him. Arthur and Clara were good people, devoted. They raised him as their own. They never told him."

The revelation hung in the air between them, vast and unyielding, a force that both tore apart and profoundly reconnected them. Sophie's mother wept, deep, guttural sobs that spoke of decades of unspoken history, of a beloved life suddenly recontextualized. Sophie held her, whispering words of comfort, of Elsie's love, of the profound sacrifice. She felt her own dry eyes finally sting with tears, a shared torrent of grief for the father they both knew, and the truth they both now shared.

A New Understanding
The raw intensity of her mother's initial shock slowly, gradually, began to subside, leaving behind a profound

weariness. They sat for a long time, side by side on the sofa, clutching each other's hands, the silence punctuated by soft sniffles and the quiet ticking of the grandfather clock in the hall. The air in the room, once charged with tension, now felt thick with shared sorrow and a burgeoning, fragile understanding.

"All these years," her mother finally murmured, her voice hoarse, her gaze fixed on the baby booties. "Edward... my Edward. He loved those photographs of Arthur and Clara. He loved his life with them. He never once hinted. Never a single question." Her voice was laced with a strange, bittersweet blend of disbelief and immense sadness.

"He couldn't have known, Mum," Sophie said gently, reinforcing the narrative Elsie had set forth. "Elsie hid it for his protection. For a chance at a good life. It was a different time. A hard time."

Her mother nodded slowly, tears still tracking lines through the pallor of her cheeks. "Elsie... your great-aunt Elsie. I always thought she was just a bit... peculiar. So quiet. Always alone. I never imagined." She looked at Sophie, her eyes wide with a new, dawning understanding. "She carried this, Sophie. All those years. This immense secret. For her son. For him to have a life without shame."

The realization of Elsie's incredible burden seemed to shift something fundamental in her mother. The reclusive aunt, once a distant, almost forgotten figure, was now transformed into a woman of immense strength, profound love, and devastating sacrifice. A new empathy bloomed in her mother's eyes, a connection across generations that bypassed all the previous silences.

"She started writing a book about it, Mum," Sophie said, her voice quiet, careful. "About Elsie and Thomas. About their story. All the letters she wrote to him. The life they built, however briefly. And the child she had to let go. I... I'm going to finish it. For her. For them. For Dad."

Her mother looked at her, her eyes searching Sophie's face. A hesitant, almost imperceptible nod. "Yes, darling. Yes. That's... that's a good idea. A very good idea. Their story deserves to be told. Edward... he would have wanted to know, wouldn't he? To know that kind of love. To know about her. About Thomas." The words, spoken with a mixture of sorrow and a newfound clarity, were a profound validation for Sophie. Her mother, too, was beginning the journey of re-evaluating their past, of integrating this new, astonishing truth.

They spent the rest of the afternoon poring over the documents together, the scanned copies of Elsie's letters, the adoption record, Thomas's last heartbreaking note. Sophie explained the details Ben had helped her uncover, the historical context of wartime adoptions, the difficulties of tracing records. Her mother listened intently, asking questions, her initial shock slowly giving way to a more profound, contemplative understanding. It was the first time they had truly connected in weeks, their shared grief for her father now augmented by a shared history, a new family secret that bound them closer.

Later that evening, after a quiet, subdued supper, Sophie called Ben. She stepped into the hallway, leaving her mother in the kitchen, still lost in thought over the letters.

"It's done," Sophie said, her voice low, a mix of exhaustion and relief.

"How did she take it?" Ben asked immediately, his voice filled with concern.

"Hard. Very hard. But... she understands. I think. She's processing it. She even thinks I should write the book. About Elsie and Thomas. And about Dad." Sophie's voice broke on the last word, the sheer weight of it catching her.

"Sophie," Ben's voice was gentle, firm. "That's huge. That's monumental. She's grieving, and yet she's open to this. That says everything about her, and about you." He paused. "Do you want me to come over? Just for a bit?"

"No," Sophie said, shaking her head, even though a part of her yearned for his grounding presence. Her mother needed her now. "Not tonight. But thank you, Ben. For everything. For helping me find this. For being... you."

"Anytime, Sophie. Anytime," he replied, and his voice held a warmth that went beyond friendship, a quiet promise of unwavering support. "Get some rest. We'll talk tomorrow. About the next steps for Elsie's story. And yours."

Sophie hung up, her hand lingering on the receiver. The conversation with her mother had been one of the hardest, most vital conversations of her life. She was exhausted, emotionally drained, but also strangely, profoundly, unburdened. The truth was out, at least to the one person who mattered most in her immediate life.

She walked back into the kitchen, where her mother sat, still holding one of Elsie's letters, her gaze distant, lost in the new reality of her husband's hidden past. Sophie sat beside her, reaching for her hand again. The cottage, Elsie's cottage, now felt truly connected to her own home, her own family. The journey of discovery was far from over, but the most difficult, most profound step, had finally been taken. And for the first time in a very long time, Sophie felt a quiet sense of purpose, a path opening before her, leading towards healing, towards creation, towards a future built on truth.

# Chapter Twenty One

The days and weeks that followed the revelation to Sophie's mother passed with a different rhythm. The raw, searing pain of her father's death began to soften, transmute into a tender ache, a profound understanding that was now inextricably linked with the astonishing truth of his birth. Her mother, initially shattered, slowly began to integrate the new narrative. The initial shock had given way to a quiet, contemplative sorrow, mingled with a strange, fierce pride in Elsie's sacrifice. Sophie found her mother often sitting by the phone, sharing fragments of the story with select, trusted relatives, her voice imbued with a newfound gravitas. The distant, reclusive Elsie Hale had transformed into a figure of quiet heroism, a woman of profound, enduring love.

Their relationship, fractured by Sophie's divorce and recent flight from London, had begun to heal, woven together by this shared, monumental secret. They spent hours together, poring over the documents, looking at Elsie's letters, and even revisiting old family photo albums with fresh eyes. Her mother would point out a distant relative, or recall a fleeting comment her father had made about his childhood that now resonated with poignant significance. "He never liked fuss, your dad," she'd say, her voice soft. "Always so self-contained. Perhaps that was Elsie's legacy, too. Her quiet strength." The conversations, once strained by unspoken grievances, now flowed freely, imbued with a newfound intimacy.

Sophie immersed herself in the book. It had begun as a quiet resolution, a personal quest to honour a hidden life, but it swiftly became a consuming passion, a therapeutic act of creation. The cottage, once a refuge from her present, was now a vibrant crucible where past and present converged. She set up her laptop in the sitting room, the fire burning brightly, and surrounded herself with Elsie's letters, Thomas's last heartbreaking note, the scanned hospital and adoption records, Ben's meticulous research notes, and now, even photographs of her father's adoptive parents, Arthur and Clara Mercer.

She started by transcribing every single one of Elsie's letters, meticulously, reverently, allowing Elsie's voice to fill the quiet rooms, to guide her. She found her own voice emerging too, intertwining Elsie's words with historical context, the insights from Ben's research, and her own raw, vulnerable reflections on love, loss, and the enduring power of secrets. The act of writing was not just an intellectual pursuit; it was an emotional excavation, a process of sifting through layers of family history, of grief, of unacknowledged truths. With each word, she felt herself shedding the skin of her old life, the person she had been with Daniel, in London, in a career that had left her hollow. This was her purpose now. This was where she truly belonged.

A Partnership Deepens
Ben remained a constant, invaluable presence. He visited frequently, navigating the sometimes treacherous, snow-covered country roads with easy familiarity. He wasn't just a research partner; he was her sounding board, her emotional support, the steady hand that grounded her when the weight of Elsie's story, or her own grief, threatened to overwhelm her. They spent hours talking, not just about the archives, but about life, about loss, about the strange paths that led people to their true callings. He brought her obscure historical texts, photocopies of wartime newspaper clippings, and fascinating details about the Home Guard units Thomas

would have been with. He'd arrive with strong coffee, and sometimes, with unexpected warmth, a tin of excellent, slightly burnt flapjacks from the café in town, a quiet joke between them.

Their professional collaboration had deepened into a profound friendship, imbued with a quiet intimacy. There were moments – a shared glance across a cluttered table, a comfortable silence stretching between them as they watched the fire, a gentle touch of his hand on her arm as she grappled with a particularly poignant letter – that spoke volumes more than words. Sophie found herself relying on his quiet strength, his unwavering belief in the importance of their work, and, increasingly, on his presence in her solitary world. She admired his intelligence, his dedication, and the gentle, respectful way he handled Elsie's sacred story. She saw in him a quiet integrity that resonated deeply with her own values, a calm steadiness that felt like a stark contrast to the volatility of her past.

One cold, clear afternoon in late winter, the sky a brilliant, startling blue after weeks of grey, Ben arrived at the cottage. He found Sophie in the sitting room, surrounded by pages of manuscript, a pen still clutched in her hand, her brow furrowed in concentration. She looked up, startled, a faint smile touching her lips.

"I think I've got it," she said, her voice filled with a quiet triumph. "The last chapter of Elsie's part. The decision to send Edward away. The final farewell in the orchard. Her unwavering belief that Thomas would come back, and her promise to him to raise their son with love, no matter what." She gestured to the pages scattered around her. "It's heartbreaking, Ben. But it's also... incredibly powerful."

Ben walked over, his eyes scanning the words on her page. He stood beside her chair, his shoulder brushing hers, and Sophie felt a familiar warmth spread through her. "It sounds like you're doing her story justice, Sophie," he murmured, his voice low, a note of deep admiration in his tone. He paused, his gaze dropping from the page to her face. "Are you doing justice to your own, though?"

Sophie looked up, surprised by the shift in his question, by the quiet intensity in his eyes. Their gazes met, and in that moment, the comfortable professional boundary between them seemed to dissolve, replaced by something far more personal, far more profound. The air in the room seemed to hum, charged with unspoken emotion.

"What do you mean?" she whispered, her heart beginning to pound a soft, urgent rhythm.

He gently reached out, his hand resting on her cheek, his thumb brushing lightly against her skin, sending a shiver through her. "I mean... are you going to keep running, Sophie? Or are you going to let yourself find a home here? Not just in the cottage, but... with this new life. With everything you've found. With..." His gaze dropped to her lips, then back to her eyes, filled with a question, a gentle invitation. "With me?"

Sophie's breath hitched. The quiet honesty of his words, the vulnerability in his gaze, was overwhelming. She had been so consumed by Elsie's past, by her father's unwritten story, that she had barely allowed herself to acknowledge the burgeoning truth in her own present. But standing here, feeling the warmth of his hand on her face, seeing the raw emotion in his eyes, she knew. This was not a distraction. This was not a temporary refuge. This was real.

"I'm not running anymore, Ben," she confessed, her voice thick with emotion, tears blurring her vision. "I haven't been running since I found Elsie's first letter. And certainly not since I met you."

He leaned closer, his eyes still searching hers, and then, slowly, gently, he kissed her. It was not rushed or demanding, but soft, tender, imbued with a quiet understanding and a shared history that was both profound and utterly new. It was a kiss of unspoken promises, of shared burdens, of futures just beginning to unfurl. Her hands found his arms, gripping him, anchoring herself to the solid reality of his presence. The weight of grief and the mysteries of the past did not disappear, but in that moment, they felt lighter, interwoven with the quiet strength of connection, of newfound hope.

Laying Ghosts to Rest
In the weeks that followed, as winter began its slow, reluctant retreat and the first tentative signs of spring painted the landscape in pale greens and soft yellows, Sophie embraced her new life. Her manuscript grew, chapter by chapter, filled with Elsie's voice, Thomas's enduring love, Edward's hidden life, and her own journey of discovery. Ben was her constant companion, her first reader, offering insights and encouragement. Their relationship deepened, settling into a comfortable, joyful rhythm of shared work, quiet evenings by the fire, and easy laughter.

One crisp morning, the air still carrying a bite of frost but infused with the promise of spring, Sophie and her mother drove to the old market town cemetery in Long Sutton. Ben joined them, a silent, respectful presence. They stood together at the grave of Arthur and Clara Mercer, the adoptive parents who had given Edward a name and a home. Sophie had brought a small, simple bouquet of white snowdrops, the first flowers of spring, picked from the cottage garden.

"Thank you," Sophie whispered, placing the flowers gently on the cold stone. "Thank you for loving him. For giving him a life." Her mother stood beside her, her hand resting on Sophie's arm, her face softened by a mixture of gratitude and sorrow. It was a moment of quiet, intergenerational reconciliation, a laying to rest of the unspoken complexities of her father's early life.

Later that afternoon, back at the cottage, with the late winter sun beginning its slow descent, Sophie walked alone to the orchard. The ancient apple trees were still bare, but their buds were visibly swelling, a vibrant green promise against the darkening bark. The earth beneath her boots was no longer frozen, but soft and yielding, absorbing the light. She walked directly to the gnarled central tree, their tree, where Elsie and Thomas had shared their last, stolen moments.

She carried nothing but a small, smooth stone, picked from the cottage doorstep. She knelt at the base of the tree, feeling the rough bark against her cheek as she leaned against the trunk. She closed her eyes, remembering Elsie's youthful strength, her fierce love. Thomas's quiet devotion, his brave, heartbreaking promise. Her father, Edward, the quiet boy who loved maps and built model ships, unknowingly carrying his true origins in his very being.

"You're not a ghost anymore, Elsie," Sophie whispered, her voice catching on a sob that was more release than sorrow. "And you're not missing, Thomas. And Dad... he's finally known."

She took out the small, worn silver locket that Thomas had carried, the one with Elsie's faded photograph, and the handful of Elsie's unsent letters, the very last ones she'd written after Thomas's final message, the ones filled with the crushing weight of her secret pregnancy. She held them for a moment, feeling their collective weight. She then placed them in a small, waterproof pouch she had prepared, and buried them carefully at the base of the tree, beneath the soft, yielding earth. A final resting place, a quiet burial for secrets that had now found their voice.

It was not about hiding them again, but about giving them a proper burial, a final, public acknowledgment, known only to her, Ben, and her mother. A private ceremony of closure.

When she returned to the cottage, the setting sun cast long, golden shadows across the kitchen floor. Ben was there, waiting, a warm, inviting presence. He looked at her, his gaze soft, understanding. He didn't need to ask what she had done. He simply opened his arms, and Sophie walked into them, letting herself be held, feeling the solid, comforting strength of him.

"It's done," she murmured against his shoulder, her voice muffled but filled with a profound sense of peace. "It's all done. And it's just beginning."

She looked out the window, at the orchard now cloaked in the soft light of dusk, its branches no longer skeletal, but holding the promise of new life. The cottage, once a place of solitude and hidden sorrows, now felt like a vibrant home, filled with the echoes of love, the peace of truth, and the quiet promise of a future, shared and open. Elsie's story was no longer lost. Her father's life was no longer incomplete. And Sophie, finally, was truly, irrevocably, home.

# Chapter Twenty Two

Two years later.

The cottage hummed with a different kind of quiet now, one that spoke of life, not just memory. The faint scent of sawdust mingled with the comforting aroma of freshly baked bread, a far cry from the dust and mothballs Sophie had first encountered. Sunlight, bright and unwavering, streamed through the newly enlarged kitchen window, bathing the worn floorboards in a golden glow. The old fireplace, once a cold, soot-stained void, now boasted a gleaming new wood burner, its warm heart a tangible centrepiece to the renovated sitting room.

Sophie leaned back against the freshly painted windowsill, a familiar weight settled comfortably against her hip: her burgeoning belly. She was six months pregnant, and the subtle, internal flutterings that had once been Elsie's secret now danced within her, a profound, undeniable link to the future. Outside, the orchard was no longer skeletal, but burst with the vibrant greens of late spring, its gnarled branches heavy with the promise of ripening fruit. The ancient apple tree, their tree, stood proud, marked now by a small, smooth stone placed reverently at its base, a silent monument to Elsie, to Thomas, to Edward.

The book sat on the windowsill beside her, its cover a muted watercolour of the cottage framed by the very orchard she gazed upon. "The Orchard Keeper's Secret: A Hidden Love Story of Wartime Lincolnshire." It had been released six months ago, a quiet success, finding its way into the hands of readers who were touched by Elsie's enduring love, Thomas's tragic fate, and Sophie's unexpected journey of discovery.

The writing had been a long, arduous, and deeply cathartic process, a way to process not just Elsie's story, but her own grief for her father, and the unraveling of her former life. Every word had been a step towards healing, a deliberate act of choosing truth over silence.

Her relationship with her mother had transformed. The initial shock had given way to a profound, shared understanding, a bond forged in the crucible of astonishing revelation. Her mother, now a frequent visitor, would sit for hours by the new wood burner, rereading Elsie's letters, tears often welling in her eyes, but always accompanied by a quiet, knowing smile. She spoke of Edward, her husband, with a new tenderness, seeing him not as someone who had kept a secret, but as a man who had lived a full, if unknowingly complex, life. She was immensely proud of Sophie's book, calling it "Edward's true legacy."

The sound of hammering drifted from the garden, a familiar, comforting rhythm. Ben. He emerged moments later, wiping sawdust from his dark blond hair, his navy jumper pushed up to his elbows. He grinned, his crooked smile dissolving the last vestiges of her London-weariness.

"Nearly done with the new shed roof," he called out, his voice warm, vibrant with purpose. He was often covered in mud, or paint, or sawdust these days. After the book was finished, Ben had quietly, unequivocally, moved into the cottage, his research now seamlessly woven into their shared life. He continued his work for the Historical Trust, but his passion for uncovering forgotten stories had found a new, deeply personal outlet in the unfolding narrative of their own lives within these old walls.

He walked over to her, his hand automatically reaching for her belly, a gentle, possessive touch that sent a familiar ripple of warmth through Sophie. "How's my little historian?" he murmured, leaning down to kiss her forehead, then her lips.

"Busy documenting the internal workings of the human body, mostly," Sophie laughed, leaning into his embrace. "And wondering about the next chapter."

He pulled up a stool, sitting beside her, his arm wrapped loosely around her shoulders. Their gaze collectively drifted around the renovated kitchen, then out to the blossoming orchard.

"It feels like home, doesn't it?" Ben said, his voice soft, contemplative. "More than just a house."

"It is home," Sophie agreed, resting her head on his shoulder. "Because we're here. And because Elsie's here. And Thomas. And Dad. All of them. Not as ghosts, but as part of the story." She paused, feeling the gentle kick within her, a quiet affirmation. "This little one will know everything. Their whole story. The love. The sacrifice. The truth."

Ben smiled, his hand moving to cover hers, resting protectively over her belly. "Every single word."

The cottage, once a quiet sanctuary for unspoken grief, now vibrated with the joy of new beginnings. The echoes of the past were no longer mournful whispers, but the foundation of a vibrant, living present. Sophie, who had fled a life that no longer felt real, had found not just a house, but a history, a purpose, a partner, and a future, all rooted in the profound, enduring power of truth and love. The silence was broken.

The story had found its voice. And the new roots were taking hold, deep and strong, in the rich Lincolnshire soil.

Printed in Dunstable, United Kingdom